KISS

REVENGE IS SWEET AN ILLUSTRATED BIOGRAPHY BY JOE STEVENS

OMNIBUS PRESS

Copyright © 1997 Omnibus Press
A Division of Book Sales Limited

Edited by Chris Charlesworth.
Cover & book designed by Michael Bell Design.
Picture research by Nikki Russell.

ISBN 0.7119.5820.3
Order No.OP47841

Exclusive Distributors:
Book Sales Limited
8/9 Frith Street, London W1V 5TZ, UK.
Music Sales Corporation
257 Park Avenue South, New York, NY 10010, USA.
Music Sales Pty Limited
120 Rothschild Avenue, Rosebery, NSW 2018, Australia.

To the Music Trade only:
Music Sales Limited
8/9 Frith Street, London W1V 5TZ, UK.

Photo credits:
Front cover: LFI; Gene Ambo/Star File: 3, 75;
Lydia Criss/Star File: 3, 75;
Max Goldstien/Star File: 90 tc,
Bob Gruen/Star File: back cover, 2, 3, 7, 12, 14, 19,
20, 27, 29b, 30, 31, 34 t, 38 inset, 43 l&br, 85, 88, 89;
Steve Joester/Star File: back cover inset, 54;
Todd Kaplan/Star File: 59 b, 74L, 87;
Bob Leafe/Star File: 63 b;
LFI: 1, 2, 3, 5, 23 b, 24, 25, 26, 28, 32, 33, 36, 37 t,
38 main, 39 t&b, 40, 41, 42, 43 tr, 44, 45, 46, 47, 48, 49,
50, 51, 52, 53, 55, 56, 57 t&b, 58 b, 59 t, 60, 61, 62,
64, 65, 72, 73, 77, 78, 79 t&b, 80, 81, 82, 83, 84, 93;
Jeff Mayer/Star File: 16, 17, 21, 22, 23 t, 29 t, 90 tl;
Ronald A.Murrey/Stare File: 69,
Chuck Pulin/Star File: 13, 15, 18, 34 b, 37 b, 57 c, 58 t;
John Ransom: 3, 66, 67, 71, 74 r, 76, 86, 90 lc&b,
90 tr, 91, 95; David Seelig/Star File: 63 t&c;
Michael Spilotro/Star File: 35.

Every effort has been made to trace the copyright
holders of the photographs in this book but one or two
were unreachable.
We would be grateful if the photographers concerned
would contact us.

Printed in Spain.

A catalogue record for this book is available from
the British Library.

Visit Omnibus Press at
http://www.musicsales.co.uk

Acknowledgements:
My thanks to the following people:
Robert Duncan - for getting me started.
John Swenson - ditto.
Chris Charlesworth - for the opportunity.
Hilary 'Cornish Blue' Power - for everything else.
Stephen Joseph - for advice, laughter and not forgetting.
Amy Joseph - the latest addition to the Kiss Army ranks.
Winona - for inspiration. Oscar beckons...
Peter at Comicana - for producing 'Hitman'
No.7 from nowhere.
Silent Bob - a role model for us all.

For additional information:
Jeff Kitts at Guitar World.
Matt Resnicoff at Musician Magazine.
R.J. Smith at Spin.
David Browne at Entertainment Weekly.
Jim Farber at New York's Daily News.

And, of course, my grateful appreciation to
the subjects of this book - Kiss.
The streets flow with the blood of non-believers...

CONTENTS

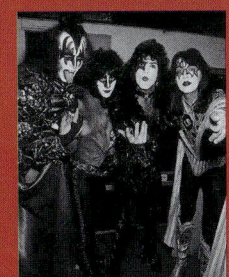

It begins with a shudder. An almost comical spasm of the shoulders. Your first reaction is to laugh. Yet, this really isn't funny at all. As the Devil in front of you begins to writhe backwards and forwards in an obscene, wretched dance, *nothing* is funny any more. That chalk-white face, that evil, leering grin. Your thoughts race. Mother. Father. Home. Anywhere but here.

★ And then it happens. Imperceptible at first, but all of a sudden frighteningly clear. There is blood in the corner of the Devil's mouth, and it's starting to drip. Down. Down his chalk-white chin. Down onto the chains binding his chest. Down towards the hungry demons that encircle his feet. You look around you, hoping for an exit. But all you can see are thousands of faces staring forward. Staring at the Devil with the bloody mouth. You avert your gaze. Pretend it isn't happening. But it's no use. The Devil is everywhere. And now his tongue is out....

★ Welcome to the wonderful world of Kiss.

In a phenomenal three-decade career, New York group Kiss have defined the blood and thunder of rock'n'roll theatre like no other band in history. A bewildering spectacle of light, darkness and all that comes between, they will forever be remembered for pushing back the boundaries of what is acceptable on a concert stage, and for many, what isn't. And they ain't finished yet.

★ A swirling contradiction of image, business savvy and out and out spectacle, Kiss have sold an astonishing *75 million albums*, played to almost as many screaming fans and, for American citizens of a particular age, been responsible for some of their most abiding dreams... and serious nightmares. Don't believe me? Here's the proof.

★ What do soul singer Stevie Wonder and thrash metal merchants Anthrax have in common? Both profess an abiding passion for Kiss. The same passion, bizarrely, that links Lenny Kravitz to Nine Inch Nails' Trent Reznor. Soundgarden's Kim Thayil says: "Kiss was the reason I started playing guitar." And he's not the only one. Ask Pantera's Dime-Bag Darrell, or Skid Row's Snake Sabo, and they'll tell you the same. Pearl Jam's six string maestro Mike McCready is the proud owner of a Kiss lunch-box: "I started playing guitar because of Kiss. To me, they were the biggest band in the world," he says without a trace of irony. Extreme's Nuno Bettencourt is of the same opinion, proclaiming: "Kiss infected me and every other kid in junior high." It doesn't stop there.

★ Punk guru Joey Ramone claims the Kiss concept was a bigger influence on American kids than the lyricism of Bob Dylan. Metallica's Lars Ulrich says that in 1977 he once found out where the band were staying, and sat outside their hotel for hours, in the vain hope of an autograph. Better still, Beastie Boy Adam Horowitz recalls that when he saw Kiss at New York's Madison Square Garden as a teenager, "I knew I'd see some action from my date." If you were young, single and awake in the Seventies, Kiss mattered.

★ Yet, despite the glowing testaments of artists as far apart as Kurt Cobain and Garth Brooks, just as many people see Kiss are a tragi-comedy in miniature, laughable geisha-dolls forever consigned to the Max Factor reject pile in the sky. Stupid. Infantile. A credibility-free zone.

★ And that is their secret.

★ Love 'em or hate 'em, you can't ignore them. And they like it that way.

★ Riding through the Seventies on a magic carpet-ride of greasepaint, explosions and fire-breathing excess, Kiss were revered and reviled in equal measure. When the original line-up split, and the make-up came off, they still sold millions of records. And still got the same dubious reviews. The mystique may have gone, the Space-Ace and Cat-Man replaced by the Black-Mane and Fox/Hawk, but they still kept coming regardless. Glam-rock, cock-rock, Love, Hate. It made no odds. Kiss were in for the long haul, no surrender.

★ And now, some fourteen years since they put the masks away, they're back. Original members. Same astonishing show. It's 1977 all over again. Alive, and in your face...

★ What follows does not purport to be an insider's guide to the secret life and times of the band. Nor is it a sycophantic treatment of a rock'n'roll legend. What it does claim to be, however, is the most accurate and honest year-by-year, blow-by-blow account of a career that has seen uncharted highs, sickening lows, tragedy, excess and more than a little magic. With Kiss there's no need to invent a story, as the facts are so strange in themselves.

★ Paul Stanley, Kiss' peerless front-man once summed up the group's singular philosophy thus: "Kiss is a life-style, it's a force, it's a pack of dogs – it's whatever you want it to be."

★ Kiss. Walt Disney for grown-ups. For astronauts. For cat-lovers. For the Devil in you. That's the beauty of these guys. You get to pick your favourite...

Facing Page:
Kiss mark two – Eric Carr,
Gene Simmons, Ace Frehley &
Paul Stanley

The Kiss story really begins in 1970, when Gene Simmons walked into Advantage Recording Studios in New York to record some of the songs he'd been playing around with. Gary Katz, Steely Dan's then producer, was working in the next room along, and as luck would have it, stopped by one afternoon to listen to what Gene was up to. So impressed was Katz by the strength of material on show that he invited the young singer/bassist to sit in on the sessions he was producing. This encouragement alone was sufficient for Simmons to seriously contemplate music as a career.

★ Up until that time, Gene had only flirted with the idea of living a rock'n'roll life. Acquiring his first guitar in his early teens ($65, a present from his mother), he'd performed in a number of garage groups such as Bullfrog Bheer, The Missing Link and Rising Sun, but his main reason for strumming chords remained predominantly below his waistline: "I never really joined... band(s) because I was interested in playing instruments. It was really a chance to meet girls. Girls were interested in rock'n'roll bands."

★ It was an interest he would indulge on an epic scale in the years to come.

★ Yet in the late Sixties, Simmons was still mindful of establishing a more conventional path in life, and therefore chose further education as his way forward. Graduating from Sullivan County Community College in upstate New York, and then Richmond College, Staten Island, he was first employed as an English teacher for fifth grade students. But when that proved harder work than he'd anticipated, the lanky Gene transferred his talents to a bewildering number of other occupations: There was the bodyguard phase. Too physical. The tenure as a typist at *Vogue* magazine. Too... precious. Rumour even had him as a night-club bouncer.

★ When none of the jobs he'd wandered into grabbed him in the same way that those three-part Beatles harmonies from across the Atlantic did, Simmons decided to indulge his fantasies – and record some tunes of his own. And that, rather neatly brings us back to the fateful moment when Gary Katz lent an ear.

★ Over the moon with the producer's positive reaction to the songs and seeing a way out of the cold comfort of a nine-to-five existence, Gene bit the bullet in January 1971, and formed his first serious band with a fellow musical friend named Stephen Coronel. He called the project Rainbow. In search of a singer/guitarist to augment their sound, Simmons and Coronel quickly put the word out among local musicians and sat back waiting for the results.

★ One of the first hopefuls to call for an audition was Paul Stanley. A recent graduate of New York's prestigious High School of Music, Stanley was brimming with confidence, and eager for an opportunity to put his talents to use. Apparently unimpressed by his credentials, and perhaps fearing an academic background was inappropriate for the rock'n'roll they had planned, Simmons and Coronel declined his offer to join the troupe. Undeterred, Paul soon turned up unannounced for one of Rainbow's sporadic rehearsals, managing to land the gig there and then. Gene would only realise later that night that this was the same guy he had rejected on the phone.

★ To add insult to injury, that occasion wasn't even the first time that Simmons and Stanley had crossed paths. Gene had actually played an impromptu show with Paul's first real band, Uncle Joe, some months before. The future Demon King might have been a whiz at literature, but it was clear his memory banks weren't working on full thrust in 1971.

★ Despite the initial hiccups, the ambitious twosome soon struck up an abiding friendship, realising they had much in common. For a start, both had recently changed their names. Gene's real name is Chaim Whitz (later Gene Klein); he was born in Haifa, Israel, on August 25, 1949. Paul Stanley is actually Stanley Eisen – well, according to his birth certificate at least – and he was born on January 20, 1950, in Queens, the New York suburb across the East River. But it wasn't just their shared age and a keen love of the opposite sex that bonded them; both shared a starry-eyed vision of what making it in a rock'n'roll band would mean to them;

★ "It meant money and girls, for sure," said Simmons, nearly 20 years later. "But mostly, it meant freedom. Freedom from the past. Freedom to do anything you wanted to with the future."

★ This freedom was surely driven by a strong immigrant work ethic. Gene had arrived in New York, with his mother (a holocaust survivor) in 1958, at the age of nine. Unable to speak the native tongue, and unsure of his new surroundings, his assimilation into American society was not easy, with bullying and playground taunts

Right:
Gene Simmons caught mugging to the camera at one of Kiss' earliest club gigs, The Daisy, February 1973
Far Right:
A formative version of Paul Stanley's 'Star Child' make-up captured in 1973
Facing Page:
Kiss mark one – Ace Frehley, Peter Criss, Gene Simmons & Paul Stanley

AND THE DEVIL FLEW INTO BROOKLYN...

from other children commonplace. Yet the young Israeli was determined to find his place, and by his teens had developed an impressive intellect and an enviable emotional body-armour, freeing him from being the butt of any further jibes. All he needed now was a direction in which to channel his energies – make his mark. Music would provide it.

★ Paul Stanley, too, had felt a sense of being apart from others, though he didn't have to travel thousands of miles to create the sensation. Sharing Simmons' Jewish background and the custom that went with it, Stanley's separation from the reality around him occurred as an adolescent when he first saw The Beatles on TV's *American Bandstand*. From that moment, the world was transformed into a different place, with a thousand new possibilities. Paul, like Gene, knew there would be no turning back. And let's face it, it sure as hell beat joining his father in the furniture trade...

★ Restless to get the show on the road, the fledgling Rainbow began rehearsing in earnest, with Gene hustling up gigs where he could find them. Any spare loft or back room bar echoed with the bombast of the trio, intent on developing their act in front of a real, live audience. As a regular following began to build, they looked to expand the line-up, experimenting with new members and sounds. Sadly, Stephen Coronel decided he'd had enough of the upheavals and quit at the end of 1971. Gene and Paul, now sensing it was time for major change, re-named the band Wicked Lester. Splitting vocal responsibilities, and placing the emphasis of their concerts much more on fun and crowd participation, the germ for Kiss was slowly starting to form.

★ This switch in tactics seemed to work, with the group soon attracting interest from the music business. A representative from Epic Records, part of the giant Columbia corporation, came down to a show one night, and impressed with what he saw, offered them a recording contract. "We thought we had it made," Simmons later recalled.

★ The Wicked Lester line-up that entered Electric Lady Studios in New York in October, 1972, to record their début album with producer Ron Johnsen was Gene on bass and vocals, Paul on rhythm guitar and vocals, Ron Leejack on lead guitar and backing vocals, Brooke Ostrander on keyboards, horn, flute and backing vocals and Tony Zarella on drums. The `WICKED LESTER` album, though never eventually released, turned out to be a dry-run for the first Kiss album. All the later hallmarks were there: manic, cackling vocals, flashy, telegraphed guitar solos, cannoning percussion and a positive gift for memorable and insistent melodies.

★ Indeed, two of the 10 tracks intended for the record – 'Love Her All I Can' and 'She' – were later re-recorded and released on the third Kiss album, *Dressed To Kill*, some three years later. There also exists a Wicked Lester version of 'Goin' Blind' which Kiss later demoed and put on their second LP, *Hotter Than Hell*, in 1974. For the record, Gene sang lead on three of the tracks: 'Simple Type', 'She', and 'Too Many Mondays', while Paul contributed vocals to 'Sweet Ophelia', 'Keep Me Waiting' and 'Love Her All I Can'.

★ Why Epic decided to pull the plug on the album after it had been recorded has never been adequately explained; the band members themselves never even receiving a complete justification – "Although we did get paid for it!" Simmons chuckled mirthlessly years later. "The music wasn't really representative of what we were doing, anyway. It wasn't hip – more like something mothers would like."

★ Whatever the reason for Epic's eleventh hour change of heart, it spelled the end of Wicked Lester as a band. (Curiously, what would have been the cover of *Wicked Lester* re-surfaced from the Columbia art file on a Laughing Dogs album, in 1979.) Deflated and shaken by the experience, Ron Leejack was first to jump ship, closely followed by Tony Zarella and Brooke Ostrander, leaving Gene and Paul to pick up the pieces. However, the duo soon noticed an ad in *Rolling Stone* magazine that read: "Drummer with 11 years' experience – will do anything to make it!" Eager to get back on the bandwagon, Simmons dialled the number straight away, and set up a meeting at Electric Ladyland. The man he would meet turned out to be Peter Criss.

★ Some three years older than Gene and Paul (he was born on December 20, 1947, in Brooklyn, New York) and considerably more experienced, Peter Criss (real name Peter Crisscoula) had previously been in a number of different jazz, rock and soul bands, most notably New York rockers Chelsea, who had recorded a self-titled album for Decca. A former gang-member of the notorious Phantom Lords (he had held the position of weapons-man), Peter had seen the musical light early enough to keep himself out of jail, and at the time of placing the ad in *Rolling Stone*, had just split from a pop outfit called Lips – keeping his chops up by playing now and then with minor Brooklyn band The Barracudas.

Right: Peter Criss before he became 'the Cat'

★ Yet it wasn't his tough disposition or Gene Krupa influenced skills behind a drum kit that got him the gig with Gene and Paul, so much as his sartorial elegance. Drowsy-eyed with just a hint of make-up, and wearing hip-hugging bell-bottomed trousers with 12-inch flares and trailing floor-length chiffon scarves, Peter showed up for his first meeting with Simmons and Stanley in the height of 1972 fashion.

★ "That day I went to... (Greenwich) Village with my brother and got really dressed, wearing this jacket I bought in England and a red satin shirt, and black velvet pants – I looked really nice. And there were these two guys – later I found out it was Gene and Paul – who had asked me (on the phone) how I dressed, standing outside the Lady with these flower shirts, looking like they came from the days of Gracie Slick and the Jefferson Airplane! I passed them up because they didn't even look like anybody. I got into Electric Ladyland and ask(ed) a guy if Gene and Paul are there and he says 'Yeah, they're right outside.' I look outside and say 'That's them?' And they asked me if I dressed!"

★ It wasn't all they had asked Criss, either. In fact, when Gene had responded to Peter's advert, he'd requested a plethora of information on the telephone – little of it relating to music. Peter expands on the tale:

★ "Gene called me while I was having a party. Everybody was smashed. I picked up the phone and he says 'Hi.'... Then he says 'Listen, first of all, are you thin?' I put the phone away from my ear and ask the party 'Hey guys, am I thin?', and everybody says 'Yeah', and I say to Gene 'Yeah, I'm thin.' Then he goes 'Do you have long hair?', and I say 'Do I have long hair?' and everybody says 'Yeah, yeah!', so I say yeah. Then he asked me if I'm good looking, and I say to everybody, 'Am I good looking?' And you could hear all these people (go) hysterical. So I say I'm really cute."

★ It was only when these life-threatening issues had been resolved, that Simmons asked his first question concerning musical experience.

★ Despite the difference in cultural and social backgrounds – Criss was Catholic, and already married – Gene and Paul immediately recognised a kindred spirit at the Electric Ladyland meeting. And after a few hastily assembled rehearsals, the pair offered him the drum spot. Suffice to say, he accepted. Reports that suggest Criss would only agree to join if Simmons and Stanley agreed to lose the shirts are without foundation.

★ For a time, the newly re-vamped Wicked Lester soldiered on as a trio, rehearsing together in a freezing loft on Manhattan's West 23rd street. By now, Gene and Paul had begun writing more and more songs together, and freed from the constraints of having to incorporate the original five-man line-up into every number, they began to break out and experiment more. Nevertheless, in order to do real justice to the songs live, they needed a full-on lead guitarist to take care of musical business. Paul would be busy singing and co-fronting the show, and the encumbrance of covering additional fretboard duties was just not on. The troupe also recognised that to evolve their ideas fully, they needed to cut all ties with the past – including the name Wicked Lester. But a new moniker wouldn't bring in the gigs the way

Wicked Lester did. It was something to be worked on.

★ Taking the attitude 'First things first' on January 3, 1973, the band placed an ad in *Village Voice*, New York's weekly news magazine, seeking a guitarist "with flash" (not "flash and balls" as stated in most articles over the years). Exactly two weeks later, a whip-thin, vampire-tall 23-year-old vision wandered into the loft in which they were rehearsing. He was wearing one red and one orange sneaker.

★ Gene recalls; "I thought a bum had walked in off the street, except he was carrying a guitar. And he walked right past us, didn't say a word... and I'm going to Paul 'Who's that? Who's this guy?'"

★ Paul takes up the story; "He basically plugged in his guitar, and just started playing. And we almost threw him out, because we said '...Who the hell are you, shut the fuck up, and sit down and wait your turn'." The enigmatic reply? "Hey, I'm sorry, Curly."

★ Yet when this weird and wonderful apparition did get his chance to jam with the band, a magic simply descended on the room. Gene knew: "This is it. This is the sound." The man who provided it was Paul 'Ace' Frehley.

A rare shot of Ace Frehley before he discovered the joys of the Gibson Les Paul guitar

★ Born in the tough streets of The Bronx – New York's northern most suburb – on April 27, 1950, Frehley was the 61st guitarist to be auditioned, but the first to be asked back. At the time he was working as a cab driver (his previous occupations having been a mailman and liquor store clerk), but Ace immediately saw a future with this promising combo, and needed little persuasion to return for a chat on the afternoon of January 22. Within minutes of arrival, he had agreed to join the ranks.

★ "When we put Kiss together," Gene recalled, "we didn't really have a clue who should be in it, or even what we should call it, but we knew what the sound was going to be. Ace and Peter were chosen because they fitted that sound."

★ Ace, influenced by British guitar legends such as Led Zeppelin's Jimmy Page and Yardbird Jeff Beck, would bring an authentic and aggressive urban stamp to the group. Sharing an immediate rapport with Peter Criss – Frehley had been a member of street gang The Hooky Boys – yet artistic enough to understand Gene and Paul's lofty goals, Ace was the perfect choice to move the dream one step closer to reality.

★ Flush with confidence, the new band re-christened themselves Kiss (the name had come to Stanley one evening as he, Gene and Peter drove down Queens Boulevard). And after a period of intense, but extremely productive rehearsals, they played their first ever show at a club called the Popcorn (re-named the Coventry on the night) in Queens, New York, on January 30, 1973. They were booked to appear for three straight nights at $30 a night, but ended up making only $70, because insufficient tickets were sold.

★ "The first show we ever did was kind of Wicked Lester; Paul and myself with new members," Gene Simmons remarked. "Back in those days, I was the one picking up the phone, dealing with printers for posters and club owners to get gigs. The truth is that we hardly had any gigs in the early days. We played at that place the Coventry in Queens twice, the Daisy (on Long Island) two or three times, then we did our own mini-concerts in New York City before we were signed."

Left to right:
The trade mark make-up evolves,
The Hotel Diplomat, July 1973

★ Despite the trouble finding venues, at least Kiss could be sure of one fact – when they hit a stage, they would be noticed. From the off, the group created a strong visual image, whether it was Simmons cavorting in sailor suits or Stanley parading shamelessly in his mother's borrowed top. To be seen was the thing, and Kiss understood it: "We wanted to stand out from the crowd," explained Simmons. "Because we didn't want to get lost among all the other young hopefuls doing the clubs in New York. Glam was big at the time, so we just took it to a logical extreme."

★ This was the era of glam-rock. Of Alice Cooper, The New York Dolls, David Bowie and T Rex. Of drag queens, fashion moths and bisexual poseurs. Trash melodies, dressed up in multi-coloured rhythms and flamboyant clothing ruled the day, and the more adventurous and outrageous you appeared, the greater your chance of taking off. And Kiss, in spite of their youth, were already well into in the game – the style, the look, the sense of dandified danger were all there. They were cavalier to the max, and prepared to make excess their creed. Mind you, attitude and finery alone would not make them an overnight sensation.

★ "The first time we played at the Coventry, we weren't even called Kiss, when I booked the band in," said Simmons. "But we did use the name for the first time that night. We had a big poster of the group in the window of the venue – a big blow-up of us looking like bad drag queens; football players trying to look like The New York Dolls. We were by no means convincing. I was actually wearing my mother's fur coat.

★ "It was embarrassing. Before the show, we decided to fool around with some make-up and we went on looking totally different to what we looked like on the poster, which Ace had just drawn the logo on... We had an audience of four: Peter's wife Lydia, the girl I was banging at the time, her brother and his girlfriend. But we just seemed blind to it all." Blind, but ambitious.

★ Over the next few months, Kiss – perhaps the ultimate in glam appellations – would play a relentless round of clubs in the New York area. Mainly, their activities centred on the Daisy, in nearby Amityville, where they appeared no less than ten times between February and April, 1973. Live, the image would congeal around a collision of tower-block shoulder-pads, gravity-defying stack-heels and full on face paint, the band still experimenting with various looks each night.

★ "The first night we played with make-up, Paul's face was all red and my face was silver," recalls Ace. "I think Gene was the first to put make-up around his eyes and wear black lipstick. Then we all decided that we should wear white faces with designs around the eyes."

★ The music too, was developing, with fans beginning to fully appreciate the Kiss sound: "There was this sense of abandon – that the stuff we were doing was working, and that it was real," recalled Simmons. "We already had songs like 'Deuce', 'Strutter', 'Nothin' To Lose', 'Firehouse'...

when people came to see us they'd say, 'Wow! This sounds like classic British stuff'. In New York then, things were very punky. Everyone had great hairstyles and looked cool, but they couldn't write songs. We were all into British stuff like Cream and The Move."

★ The reactions they were getting fuelled their ambitions still further, and in February 1973, they took it upon themselves to put together their own Kiss promo kit. Gene wrote the words and one of the band's many girlfriends took some pictures. Yet, strange to relate, none of the photos featured the band with their make-up – within the ranks the jury was still out on that particular verdict. Nevertheless, the package was sent to various clubs and agencies in the hope of drumming up interest. And as the group knew only too well, it couldn't hurt for the Kiss name to be doing the rounds – after all, any publicity was good publicity. Yet when nobody took the bait by the end of spring, it was time to go to Plan B...

★ Tight from recent gigging and anxious to get their music on tape, Kiss entered Electric Ladyland Studios on June 17,1973 with producer/engineer Eddie Kramer – famous for his work with Jimi Hendrix and Led Zeppelin – to spend two weeks recording demos. The first song to be laid down? 'Strutter', co-written by Gene and Paul. Beginning life as the oddly-titled 'Stanley The Parrot' (which doesn't quite have the same arrogant toss of the head as the monster it would become), it was nonetheless a fitting tune for their recorded debut: Loud, insistent guitars, a tight, melodic bassline, impassioned, confident vocals and a howling, vibrato driven solo all conspired to define the Kiss vibe. Add a cocky, arrogant swing to the beat, and a deceptively simple approach to harmony, and you have the complete picture.

★ Other tracks recorded at the time were Gene's marvellous stomper 'Deuce' (with lyrics even *he* admits to not understanding), 'Watchin' You' (another Simmons tune), the two-toned 'Black Diamond' (written by Paul) and the raucous, good-time ode to alcohol 'Cold Gin' (Ace's first contribution to the group, and still in the live set today). All but 'Watchin' You', which surfaced on *Hotter Than Hell*, would end up on their first disc. Contrary to popular belief, the good-time funk-rock of 'Firehouse' was not recorded during these sessions.

★ Pleased with the results, Kiss sent out their freshly minted and self-financed demo to as many record company contacts as they could muster, inviting all interested parties down to watch them perform their own self-produced show-case at the Hotel Diplomat near Times Square on July 13, 1973, with headlining act The Brats. Nobody came backstage afterwards waving a cheque book, but the gig did garner a positive review from the influential *Variety* magazine. Spirits raised, the group would perform two further showcase gigs at the Diplomat, on August 9 and 10, and among the audience this time was a former TV music show producer called Bill Aucoin whose show *Flipside* was big in the US in the late Sixties and early Seventies.

The Hotel Diplomat, August 1973

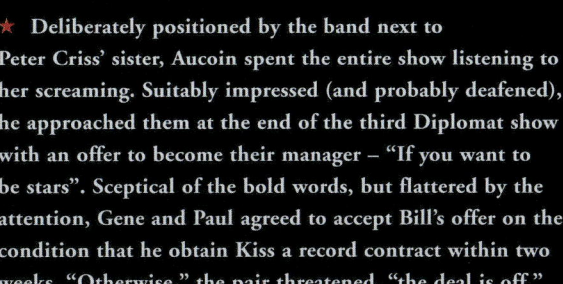

★ Deliberately positioned by the band next to Peter Criss' sister, Aucoin spent the entire show listening to her screaming. Suitably impressed (and probably deafened), he approached them at the end of the third Diplomat show with an offer to become their manager – "If you want to be stars". Sceptical of the bold words, but flattered by the attention, Gene and Paul agreed to accept Bill's offer on the condition that he obtain Kiss a record contract within two weeks. "Otherwise," the pair threatened, "the deal is off."

★ Good as his word, Aucoin came through with the offer of a record deal on August 24, 1973. He had been to see Neil Bogart, head of Casablanca Records, who agreed to sign Kiss on the strength of their demo. The quartet could hardly believe what they were hearing. Was this guy on the level? Apparently so...

★ "We got a deal on the strength of a demo," recalls Simmons. "Neil Bogart had never even seen a photo of us, so when we came to see him he thought we were great, but didn't want us to wear make-up. We told him: 'Take it or leave it'. We had our vision – and it took balls to tell him that, 'cos we didn't have any money. Once Neil saw the madness of it all, he gave us $250,000 worth of special effects, hanging Kiss logos and everything. People soon began to fall victim to the crusade and our show became the circus that everyone would flock to see once it marched into town."

one of Bogart's partners in the early days of Casablanca, would later recall: "If it cost him three dollars to make two dollars, he would do it."

★ It was this attitude of 'excess equals success' that would perfectly complement the outrageous antics of his first major signing. Casablanca were the first ever label staffed entirely by promotions people, a move unprecedented at the time, and when the company was launched, Bogart spent $50,000 on a party at New York's Century Plaza Hotel's grand ballroom, which he had redecorated to look like the set from the movie *Casablanca*. To give a further indication of the man's style, to promote Donna Summer's first hit album in the US, *Love To Love You Baby*,

★ Casablanca Records would eventually become a glittering home not just to Kiss, but also to artists like Donna Summer, Cher, and The Village People, as well as the 'nearly made it' hard rock act Angel, one of many acts Simmons would discover over the years. Its plush offices were along fashionable Sunset Boulevard in West Hollywood, and outside in the street would sit a dozen or more Mercedes cars, usually convertibles. Anyone who subscribed to the American Dream, LA-style, in the Seventies, required a Merc, and Casablanca – built largely on the sales of Kiss – would embody that dream like no other American record label before it, nor perhaps since.

★ Its boss and leading light was legendary. By the time Neil Bogart died at the age of 39 from cancer of the kidney and colon – a condition possibly aggravated by extensive drug abuse – he was a man for whom the expression 'Whatever It Takes' had become a credo. As Art Kass,

Bogart held a special party for her in New York, for which a life-size cake *sculpted in the singer's image* was made in Los Angeles and flown to New York in two first-class airline seats. Met by a freezer ambulance at the airport, the cake was driven to the party just in time for Summer's appearance. "Spend, parties, promotion, fly jockeys in, hire 25 promotion men. Whatever it took," recalled one industry insider from those days. "He was a mover and shaker; there was nobody like Neil."

★ Curly-haired and cherub-faced, he was born Neil Bogatz, in Brooklyn, in 1943, the son of a postal worker and a mother who ran a foster home. He would later refine his name at the age of 18, when he was accepted into the New York School of Performing Arts – the TV Fame school – as a singer and dancer. Choosing soon after to pursue a career in music, Bogart was signed as a vocalist to Portrait Records, for whom he made a handful of singles, only one of which – a dewy-eyed ballad called 'Bobby' – ever made the charts. It reached No.58 in the US in 1962, selling about 200,000 copies in the process.

★ Unable to duplicate the success of 'Bobby' but wishing to continue his association with music, Bogart next wrangled himself a job as an ad salesman for *Cash Box*, a US trade magazine, but it was only when he moved to MCA Records as a promoter that he found his true vocation in life. Not as a record maker, but as a record seller.

★ His natural aptitude for promotional work led in 1967 to a high-powered position at the independent Cameo Parkway Records in Philadelphia, and his first decision – to sign the strangely named ? And The Mysterians – led to a huge international hit in '96 Tears', a classic of the garage genre. From there, he went to become general manager of Buddha Records, where he enjoyed even more good fortune with two of the biggest bubblegum pop acts of the Sixties; Ohio Express and 1910 Fruitgum Company, both of which, in reality, were comprised entirely of session musicians. Indeed, both 'groups' even had the same lead singer, Joey Levine.

★ In 1973 Bogart finally got what he had wanted all along: his own record company. Christened Casablanca in honour of the timeless movie of the same name (and starring that other famous Bogart), it would allow Neil total control of the decision-making process, with the power to hire and fire his own acts. With luck (and God-given business sense) one of the first moves he made was to sign Kiss and, convinced that the group's visual image was crucial to their potential, he regularly frequented magic shops to load up on special effects, adding the new toys to the group's ever growing theatrical arsenal. Bogart even went as far as hiring Amaze-O the Magician to demonstrate to Gene Simmons the art of fire-breathing for future stage use. Yet, when Gene tried to duplicate one of Amaze-O's stunts, the usual Kiss confidence seemed temporarily to disappear, as everyone – including Neil – dived behind the couch in his office in abject fear!

★ Still, much taken by his first real hard rock signing and stirred by Bill Aucoin's business savvy and ambitious plans for the group, Bogart soon attended a meeting at Casablanca distributors Warner Brothers declaring, "Kiss is magic!", sending a puff of smoke from his hand to seal the image. With this mogul behind them, and the canny intelligence of Aucoin steering the management ship, it could only be a matter of time before stardom came calling. Years later Ace Frehley would acknowledge the debt: "Bill and Neil were the real geniuses... I think it was really the management that was responsible for making the band happen."

★ Still, back in 1973, Kiss were only just beginning to build a regular following through the hard slog of playing live. On August 31, they started a three-night stint back at the Coventry, with opening act Wild Honey in tow, the first of many such gigs around the New York area. But while the shows might have been small time, they were all part of the policy of refining their material and establishing a solid base – aims critically important to a newly signed group. Casablanca saw Kiss as having the potential to be global stars, and the band were not about to argue. But first, there was work, work and more work. Only when you could hear a pin drop between drum-beats, would they be ready to cut their début album.

★ The chance finally came on October 10, when the band entered Bell Sound Studios, near 57th street in Manhattan, to begin the process of capturing their vibe on record. With Kenny Kerner and Richie Wise producing, Kiss worked steadily for about a month on basic song structures before turning their attention to overdubs and mixing down the tracks, a process that would see out the year. In addition, the band were also gainfully employed revamping their stage show, adding various props and tools, to ready it for a jump up the ladder from small-time unknowns to major players. In a symbolic gesture of 'farewell', they performed their last shows at the Coventry on the 21st, 22nd and 23rd of December, 1973. It was soon to be hit or bust time.

★ Nevertheless, on December 31, Kiss received something of an antidote to any pre-record release fears, when they were asked to appear at a special New Year's Eve party at the New York Academy Of Music. Opening for Blue Öyster Cult, Iggy Pop & The Stooges, Teenage Lust, as well as a German oom-pah band from Luchow's Restaurant next door (whom BÖC hauled on stage to add a surreal air to the bash), it was an ideal opportunity to let their hair down and relax into the New Year.

★ Unfortunately, Gene took it a little too far, igniting his locks during a fire-breathing stint at the end of 'Firehouse'. Still, he had some famous shoulders to cry on backstage, as Todd Rundgren and Rick Derringer commiserated with his plight and cautioned the young pup against playing with fire in the future. It would be a lesson the adventurous bassist would seldom heed.

★ On the live front, Ace was fast becoming a major star in the show. The fragile guitarist would prowl Kiss' exploding stage like a stoned phantom, Les Paul in hand, with the unmistakable vibrato of his abrasive solos adding immeasurably to the whole Kiss encounter. Never one for formal theory (he had honed his chops in power-combos such as Molimo and Four Roses before joining Gene and Co.), Ace had developed his unique style of squeezing notes from the fretboard not by shaking the string itself – but the whole guitar too!

Gene Simmons' famous candelabra (far left)

★ "I didn't know shit from shineola," he laughed later, "(but) I think that's one of the reasons that I'm original."

★ An adventurous and instinctive player, Ace's bold and otherworldly approach was well represented at the time, with the strange, chance-taking leads that glorified tracks like 'Strutter', '100,000 Years' and 'Firehouse.' Abandoning established technique in favour of wild inventiveness, Frehley's solo flights personified the whole group's willingness to push back any boundaries that restricted them.

★ Kiss in concert, however, was by no means the Ace Frehley Experience. Paul and Gene had also become barn-storming show-men, acting as dual masters of ceremony while treading the boards. Whipping up the punters with their heady cocktail of sex and horror, the terrible twosome exhibited all the signs of stardom: arrogance, charisma and pure balls. With Peter holding down a ferocious backbeat, and adding impassioned, throaty vocals to the light and shade of 'Black Diamond', all four members truly earned their keep.

★ The band's first album, simply titled `KISS` was

finally released by Casablanca Records on February 8, 1974.

Featuring the group in full make-up on its jet black cover,

the LP now stands up rather well to the test of time,

combining a certain glam rock charm with real powerchord

riffage. Paul Stanley's vocal style, even in those far-off,

formative days, had a certain seductive, smooth charm,

while Gene Simmons provided his soon-to-be trademark

rasp and raunch to the grittier tracks.

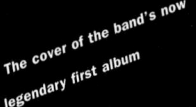

The cover of the band's now legendary first album

★ With the sprawling musical romanticism of 'Black Diamond', the celebratory groove of 'Firehouse', the insouciant arrogance of 'strutter' and the humorous swagger of 'Cold Gin', the record introduced four absolute Kiss classics to the world, and defined their grasp of blood and thunder. In addition, 'Kissin' Time' – another track to make the début disc – suggested that the group could pen those

all-important 'crossover' hits, reeking as it was with radio friendliness. Mind you, the original version of *Kiss* didn't even feature the tune, with the band content to record it only as a promo for radio station WSHE in Fort Lauderdale, Florida. It was to be added to the album later (much against the group's wishes) by Neil Bogart, who saw its potential pop appeal.

★ It wasn't the last re-jigging the record would see. When *Kiss* was re-issued by PolyGram in the early Eighties, the studio version of 'Nothin' To Lose' would be replaced with the live one from *Alive!*. Incidentially, the track 'Let Me Know', featured on the disc, was originally titled 'Sunday Driver' – and was the first song to be played by Paul to Gene when they initially met. 'Love Theme From Kiss' was also recorded under the title of 'Acrobat'.

★ To accompany the album's release, Neil Bogart hired the expensive Century Plaza Hotel in Los Angeles for a major blow-out, turning it into 'Rick's Café' from the film *Casablanca* for the night. The place was packed, and guests included the king of shock-rock himself, Alice Cooper. "They're a good band. All these guys need is a gimmick," he mischievously told reporters. Meanwhile, back in New York, Kiss hired the shuttered and closed Filmore East for a press show/party to launch the album on the East Coast of America. No expense, it seemed, spared.

★ *Kiss* was also backed up with a nation-wide kissing competition as the nub of a major US promotional campaign. But despite all the furore surrounding its release, the album only made No.87 in the *Billboard* charts – although it did stay around for a total of 23 weeks. The potential hit single, 'Kissin' Time', was also put out in an effort to boost sales, but when it only went as high as No.83 in June 1974, hopes of platinum success were stalled.

★ Still, at least the band had dented the charts and begun the march to stardom. And if they couldn't afford the greatest show on earth just yet, then they'd have to improvise: "We knew what we wanted to be long before we could afford to be it," said Paul "In the beginning, we saw these great chrome drums, but we couldn't afford them. So we went to Canal Street and bought adhesive Mylar. It's kinda like wallpaper. And we took all the lugs off the drums and Mylared everything to make them look expensive. I also made Gene's and my first pair of stage pants. The pants we wanted were made with this metallic-type fabric, Lurex. They were $35 a pair. They might as well have been $3,500. So I went out and bought some fabric. I took apart my favourite pair of jeans, made patterns – God knows how! – and sewed these trousers. I had never worked a sewing machine in my life. My mother said, 'You'll never be able to put the zippers in'. Being a complete idiot, I just sewed them in somehow."

★ Simmons adds to the story: "We always had to improvise. We wanted leather guitar straps with studs on them and neck collars with studs. We couldn't find studded leather guitar straps so we used belts from the S&M shops in the Village. We'd walk into the Pleasure Chest or Eagle's Nest, a potpourri of pleasure and pain, and stare at stuff on the wall, trying to figure out how to use it on stage."

★ For Paul and Gene, being in Kiss wasn't just about being rock stars. It was their life. They would turn up to gigs extra early to set up so people wouldn't know they didn't have roadies. And they surreptitiously plastered posters up in the middle of the night and let people believe it was the work of fans or employees."

★ "We never wanted anyone to know that we were the driving force behind the band," recalled Paul. "But we weren't a bunch of guys willing to wait for people to do things for us. We've always been self-contained, and we realised nobody could do it better than us."

★ What was setting the band apart from any of their rivals were those costumes and that face-paint. The costumes grew out each member's personal fantasies – comic books, science fiction, monster movies. But what about the makeup? That must surely have been a pretty risky manoeuvre for a macho bunch of New York rock'n'rollers:

★ "People ask us who our role models were, but none of them were musical," Simmons once explained. "After we figured out the costumes and staging, we just kept taking it a little further. One night, we just started putting make-up on. Nobody was cracking up. It was very nonchalant, like, 'OK, it's time to put make-up on'. Our vibe was: 'Let's go where no band has gone before'. Before Peter joined the band, one of the first questions we asked him was: 'Are you willing to do anything? If necessary, are you willing to put on a dress?' We knew we were going to go out there."

★ From the earliest days, Kiss exuded an air of total confidence in their footpadding to the top. Nothing seemed to knock this inner determination and focus. Criticism? Water off a duck's back. As Simmons attests now, they simply didn't care if people around them had a problem with their one-track collective.

★ "I remember we were doing some session work on an obscure record at a recording studio, and we ran into Garland Jeffries, who already had a couple of records out. We had maybe played two gigs in our lives at that point. But we're walking along with the Kiss logo on our guitar cases and he says, 'Who are you?' We said, 'We're stars'. His reaction was 'Whaaaa?'"

★ "We didn't say it arrogantly, just matter-of-fact," adds Paul. "We believed there was no way we would fail. Anything that got in the way was going to be trampled."

★ And this included the bands whom Kiss supported in those early days. They were not immune to this utterly ruthless grind, as Gene laughingly recalls. "Those poor headlining bands that took us out on the road – we pitied them! Ha. We loved the bands, but we were determined to destroy them. And we did. You'd see their carcasses litter the stage. I remember Argent would never let us play encores. They would pull the power. But one night, they didn't pull the power, and we kept playing. We ran out of songs and just started repeating them. Later we found out our crew had locked Argent's road manager in an equipment case. We were thrown off the tour."

★ Years later all seemed to be forgiven when Kiss covered the classic Argent song 'God Gave Rock 'N' Roll To You' and turned it into a monster hit. But make no mistake, if you took out Kiss as your opening act, be prepared for severe mental scars – they were out for blood every time they hit the stage.

★ From February-April 1974, the groups who had to deal with just that problem were Manfred Mann's Earth Band and Savoy Brown – the former a musicianly troupe based around veteran South African keyboardist Manfred Mann, the latter a rugged rock/blues combo. Strange choices indeed to pair with New York's premier glam experience. Neither could hope to compete with a hungry, venomous Kiss, armed as they were with $100,000 worth of new equipment and a million dollar attitude.

★ "Our belief in ourselves was contagious," confirmed Paul. Nothing would stand in their way – not even the public's lukewarm response to their recorded début. They would fall to their knees in supplication eventually. All that was needed was a little coaxing.

Ace Frehley feels the burn

After extensive touring on the back of their début LP, Kiss returned to the studio in the Autumn of 1974 to begin work on what would become their second album – 'HOTTER THAN HELL' Confident of the new material they had written on the road, and spurred on by the stunned reaction of audiences to their increasingly spectacular stage show, their spirits were high during the recording sessions, and the band were cocked and loaded for impending success. It must have been a crushing blow to them when the album, released in November, was greeted with a muted commercial and critical response. Crushing, and indeed strange, considering of how good it was...

★ Produced by **Kenny Kerner** and Richie Wise at Village Recorder Studios in Los Angeles, *Hotter Than Hell* proved a winning combination of light and shade, full of hard-rock bluster and gyrating pop. Coming ever closer to fulfilling Simmons' vision of "A heavy metal Beatles", songs such as 'Got To Choose', 'All The Way' and 'Comin' Home' bristled with energy and tunefulness, while 'Parasite', 'Watching You' and the LP's title track resounded with grinding, insolent

menace. Perhaps the best way of illustrating the album's dual approach though, was by contrasting two of its stand-out moments – 'Strange Ways' and 'Goin' Blind'.

★ The former tune, written by Frehley, was a vicious, cut-throat rocker, slow in pace, and featuring a mind-boggling solo from the guitarist. Simmons' 'Goin' Blind', on the other hand, was a gentle, evocative ballad, swirling in chord changes and soaring vocal harmonies. Bombast and harmony, power and sophistication. Yet, it still wasn't enough for the US record buying public, who accorded the release an even worse showing than the group's début LP. *Hotter Than Hell* stiffed at No.100 on *Billboard*.

★ Nevertheless, at least one country bought into the album, albeit for its cover. The Japanese, perceiving the disc's cod-oriental sleeve to be a homage to their culture, showed their generosity by buying *Hotter Than Hell* in droves – thereby turning it into a hit in the lucrative Far-Eastern market. Cynics may have shouted "Marketing ploy!" at Kiss until they were blue in the face, but it was the beginning of a faithful and abiding relationship between Japan and the band that still exists today.

★ If Kiss' albums weren't exactly setting the world on fire this side of the Orient, then at least the band's attention-grabbing make-up was paying dividends. Those kabuki-like black and white ghosts of their earliest days were now fully developed personalities – Simmons a lascivious Demon with bat-wings for a face, Stanley the all-loving Star Child with an obsidian twinkle adorning his right eye, Frehley a psychedelic Space Ace, frail and aloof, Criss a grinning Cat with pan-stick whiskers – and an increasing number of punters were being drawn to the concert shows to see just what the hell was going on.

★ Paul Stanley, of course, had his own take on things. "Like all great things, it came from the darkest recesses of the soul. The make-up was never really thought about, it just happened. Each one of us obviously got in touch with something inside ourselves, which is what made it genuine. If some other band tried it, they looked like fools."

★ "I've always felt like a stranger in a strange land," adds Simmons. "I was an Israeli before I came to America, and when I arrived I had this wonder with all things American. Everything was bigger, even the people. As a child, I became obsessed with comics, movies and rock'n'roll, and the first time I put the make-up on, what came out and how I moved on stage was a combination of all the images that fascinated me, from *The Phantom Of The Opera* (the original with Lon Chaney) and *Batman* to *King Kong* and (Hungarian actor) Bela Lugosi (regarded as the greatest screen Dracula of them all)."

★ "All four of us were so over the top personalities that it was important for each person to define themselves," Stanley expanded. "From the day Ace walked into an audition wearing one red sneaker and one orange one, it was obvious to the rest of us that he was very spacey. He'd talk about this mythical planet called Jendell that existed in his head. Peter, meantime, liked to think of himself as somebody who, like a cat, had nine lives. Somebody who grew up on the street, took chances and had gotten away with a lot."

The cover to 'Hotter Than Hell'
Note the oriental design
Facing Page:
"Are you talking to me?"

THANK GOD FOR DETROIT

Gene Simmons' neck muscles temporarily desert him

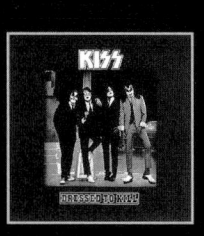

Kiss' third album 'Dressed To Kill'

★ Criss, perhaps of all the members of Kiss, embraced the latent power of those ghostly images: "Look at this face" he says of his feline fissog today, "That's a gift from God... I often ask myself 'Where did that come from?' I could have been a fox, or a bear... but this is me! For some reason I feel so comfortable with this... I'm serious about it. It's not just a gimmick... this is a reality."

★ Unfortunately though, the show that had been developed to accompany the extraordinary face-paint was proving hugely expensive to maintain. With the widespread use of smoke bombs to accent key moments in the set, police-lights blazing throughout the house during 'Firehouse', and a huge, bulb-eating logo pulsating behind the group, dollars were being burned away nightly, and tickets for the circus could only recover some of them. Therefore it was critical for Kiss that record sales took off. And soon.

★ Painfully aware of the financial pressure, the band wasted little time getting stuck in to their next studio project. Within five months of *Hotter Than Hell* hitting the shops, they were back in New York's Electric Ladyland, co-producing their third record with label boss Neil Bogart.

★ The result **'DRESSED TO KILL'** was to prove more accessible than either of its predecessors, although it still had a hard, occasionally harsh edge. Paul Stanley provided pop sleaze with the album opener 'Room Service' (A twilight tale of the rock'n'roll lifestyle delivered with trademark panache), while Simmons' 'Two Timer' kept up the pace, illustrating the quartet's growing confidence with melody and tempo. Other highlights included the three-minute wonder 'C'mon

And Love Me', with its brash, lyrical insolence, and future crowd-pleaser 'She', slow burning and guitar heavy. But of course, the real gem on the LP was a teen anthem in the making – 'Rock And Roll All Nite'. Loud, up-tempo party music, with a chorus so simplistic it must have been divinely inspired, the song would soon carry the flag for the Kiss revolution.

★ *Dressed To Kill*'s album sleeve once again provided a talking point for fans, seeing the band (still in full make-up), wearing smart, sharp suits on a city street – Ace, laconic as ever, leaning against a lamppost. The image was captured just outside Electric Ladyland by photographer Bob Gruen on completion of recording, and trivia fiends might be interested to know that it was the very last photo taken in this session that provided the cover. Don't know about Gene's clogs though.

★ *Dressed To Kill* gave Kiss their best chart placing thus far, with the LP reaching a respectable No. 32 in the US charts on its release in April, 1975. The single chosen to be the lead-off track, inevitably the mob shin-kicker 'Rock and Roll All Nite' (originally titled 'Drive Me Wild'), was put out in May and reached No. 68. It would return soon however, with a bang.

★ On the verge of hitting the big time, but still tantalisingly short of pay-dirt, Kiss next played a master stroke. Detroit had become a big market for them and they were to count on their fan-base there to help them up the next rung on the ladder to success. "We were doing very well as a live band, but just not selling any records," Paul Stanley recalled. "So Casablanca decided to see if they could use our live success to sell records. It worked. If it hadn't, I don't know what would have happened."

★ While Stanley may have sounded dramatic, his words were uncomfortably accurate. The record label had sunk hundreds of thousands of dollars into Kiss by this point, and funds were running out. Even though

Dressed To Kill had performed reasonably well chart-wise, its sales couldn't hope to recoup previous spending and drastic measures were in order. Kiss, Bogart and Aucoin decided to gamble, a live LP was the stake.

★ With the release of the concert performance recorded at Detroit's Cobo Hall (with some tracks also being gleaned from Cleveland and New Jersey), Kiss finally broke down America's door for good. The record 'ALIVE!' captured the band in all their pomp and glory, and allowed record buyers everywhere a taste of the Kiss live experience. Produced by Eddie Kramer, and featuring a startling, multi-coloured image of the group in full show-stopping swing on its cover, the 16 songs present pulsated with rough-hewn life and spirit.

★ As fresh and vibrant today as it was two decades ago, 'Alive!' remains a landmark in the history of American rock 'n' roll. Opening with the fierce charge of the Simmons penned 'Deuce', Kiss continued to build the pressure with a testosterone-laced 'Strutter', before really hitting hard with the winning trio of 'Got To Choose', 'Hotter Than Hell' and 'Firehouse' – sirens blaring from the speaker grilles at the latter song's conclusion. After this aural assault, the rather ordinary 'Nothin' To Lose' dampened proceedings somewhat, but a blistering one-two combination of 'C'mon And Love Me' and 'Parasite' got the band and audience back into a real unified groove. 'She', next up, proved

somewhat sombre and precious (despite a smoking solo guitar showcase from Frehley) and dropped the pace slightly, though 'Watchin' You' and '100,000 Years' opened the second record in bold and brash fashion – immediately re-stoking the theatrical fires. Next on the hit-list was a lively 'Black Diamond' whose numerous switches in mood and tempo positively fizzed in a live setting, before it gave way to the basic and anthemic chug of 'Rock Bottom'. Recovery was swift with the instrumental pyrotechnics of Ace's 'Cold Gin', before 'Rock And Roll All Nite' marched on, threatening to take the roof off the hall. Annoyingly simple it may have been, but when it came to getting a city on its feet, few songs touch it. Finally, there was the good-time boogie of 'Let Me Go Rock 'N' Roll', which tended toward anti-climax after the scintillating stride of its predecessor. Perhaps Kiss left it on the LP to ensure nobody listening died of a heart attack before the needle lifted from the grooves!

★ Overall, *Alive!* was almost a 'Best Of' package, designed to coerce a hitherto unconvinced public into becoming part of the growing Kiss Army. And boy, did it do the trick. When *Alive!* hit the racks in November 1975, it catapulted straight to No. 9 in the US charts, and a re-issued version of 'Rock And Roll All Nite' (from *Alive!*) sealed the victory when it rose to No. 12 in the singles roster – 56 places higher than on its original release. The band had made the transition from a top concert attraction to top-notch record shifters, and saved themselves and their record company by doing it. Now the serious business of having fun could begin. And if up until now Kiss had been studiously ignored by the majority, with the success of *Alive!* they could bring the party to almost every house in the USA.

★ Sealing their newly acquired star status, on February 20, 1976, the band were honoured when they flew to Hollywood to have their footprints placed in concrete outside the world famous Grumman's Chinese Theatre. Kiss joined a legendary list of entertainers, such as Marliyn Monroe, Frank Sinatra and James Stewart who had been so immortalised. Naturally, the group turned up in full make-up and on-stage regalia. They now went nowhere in public without them.

★ "Not being photographed without make-up was something that happened accidentally," Simmons claimed. "The press felt we were hiding our real identities, which wasn't the case. They wanted to know what we really looked like, and from then on the make-up became almost religious. We felt we were becoming much more than a rock'n'roll band. We gained a sense of power in the same way women feel more powerful and attractive with make-up on. Once we were caught in the press' fascination with it, we decided to keep out of the limelight. It did become a 24-hours-a-day pain in the ass. And, at one point there was a $25,000 reward out for anyone who could take a picture of me without my make-up on."

★ Yet, they could hardly complain about the pan-stick. After all, their larger than life image had been a major weapon in their eventual success, and it would have been discourteous for the group to begrudge their fate. Paul Stanley summed it up thus: "That's like winning the lottery, and then complaining about the taxes... If you're lucky enough to get what you wanted, shut up."

★ By mid-1976, Kiss was just about the biggest home-grown rock band in America, giving friendly rivals Aerosmith and ZZ Top a run for their money, and Casablanca had swollen to one of the USA's biggest labels. The company payroll had risen from 14 full-time employees in 1973 to nearly 200 by the time Kiss were collecting their first platinum records, and the success was having all manner of effects. "At three o'clock in the afternoon, an adorable little girl would come up and take your order for the following day's drug supply," recalled Danny Davis, former Phil Spector promotion man who worked at Casablanca at the height of Kissmania. Pizzas, presumably, were even easier to secure.

★ For a time, it seemed that everything Kiss and/or Casablanca touched turned to gold (or more often than not, platinum. Or multi-platinum, come to think of it). As Gene Simmons noted only half-jokingly at the time: "The only possibility of anything going wrong is the band blowing itself up!"

★ Paul Stanley: "*Alive!* broke at the right time, because we were broke and so were the record label, Casablanca. Our record sales were pretty soft, but we were building this huge reputation as a live band. We figured that either people didn't like the records or else they didn't capture what we were like live. We felt that we needed to give people a souvenir of the live show.

★ "When we were doing *Alive!*, the only thing we had for intensity was our own sweat and blood. Success gave us the ability to dream something up and then ask someone to build it. Every time we went on tour we tried to add something, get ourselves off as much as our fans. We'd give people what they didn't see elsewhere. I mean, you'd be hard pressed to come up with a better ending to a show than what you see on the gate-fold sleeve to *Alive II*."

★ But we're getting ahead of ourselves a little here. There's still the matter of promotion to talk about first...

Left:
A passer-by is suitably impressed by the size of Gene's codpiece
Facing Page:
The most famous tongue in rock

Paul, what's your favourite food? "Soup and sweets."
Gene, what's your favourite colour? "Black."

If the interviewer had asked, however, what their favourite possession was, there would have been one clear and unified response: Money.

★ By 1976/77, Kiss were marketing themselves on a scale larger than anything ever seen in rock'n'roll before. Their highly visual image offered a unique opportunity to sell group-related commodities to millions of fans all over the world, and they went for it – lock, stock and barrel. Ruthlessly plundering the profits from their non-musical efforts, they virtually invented the modern concept of rock merchandising – a way in which bands of all hues can reap gigantic rewards from selling all manner of related ephemera – and became multi-millionaires in the process.

★ Years later, these lessons were keenly learned and improved upon by countless money-minded Eighties rockers. Iron Maiden, for example, became immeasurably rich from the profits of their merchandising operation long before the sales of their albums. Building a cult around the ghoulish figure of 'Eddie' – a mummified monster depicted on all the band's album sleeves and singles – the East-London metallers reaped lavish rewards from T-shirt sales across the globe. Canadian prog-rockers Rush only ever agreed to tour the UK because they knew they would make a killing on T-shirts and swag. And even today's most steely raconteurs, Oasis, must surely have inadvertently learned a thing or two from the Kiss operation, with their image now becoming increasingly hard to escape on every city street.

★ As the Seventies entered their dotage, Kiss lunch-boxes, Kiss lawn-mowers, Kiss pinball machines and even Kiss children's make-up became commonplace in the US. There were even plans hatched for a Kiss punch-bag, if you can believe it! Under the effective guidance of manager Bill Aucoin, the group were, at one point, making more money from their non-musical endeavours than anything else. In fact, by 1978, they were even quoted as being the fifth largest corporation in America – evidence, if any were still needed, that this was a band who were also the most astute of businessmen.

★ "Bill stepped in after we'd become a pretty big band in New York. We were already wearing make-up, we had the logo (patented, of course) and had actually written all the songs for the first two albums," Paul Stanley said of Aucoin's role in the band's success. "At times he is like another member, but in the end it's still Kiss that runs Kiss, and we know better than anybody what's best for us."

★ True, but it was increasingly hard to underestimate the importance of Aucoin's genius for promotion, as Kiss dolls – "each sold separately" – flooded the stores, becoming the object for pre-pubescents everywhere. "Put them in any crazy pose you want!" screamed the advertisements. Umm... thanks, but no.

★ Though Aucoin would tragically die of AIDS before the group's astonishing resurrection of the mid-Nineties (Kiss' management reins subsequently transferring to New York company Glickman/Marks in the early Eighties), his unique ideas on how to market musical acts are still a lesson to up-and-coming svengalis the world over. Understanding his charges to be 50% rock'n'roll band, 50% fantasy, Aucoin and partner in crime Neil Bogart sold Kiss to that gaping black hole in the teenage psyche – wish fulfillment. Bored with your schoolbooks? Getting a hard time from the kids on your block? The girl of your dreams still ignoring you? Come voyage around the stars with Kiss! Escape your worries, your doubts, those ogres you call parents. Take 'Christine Sixteen' in your arms and join the 'Rocket Ride' to Kissland!

★ Like those great media manipulators before him – The Rolling Stones' Andrew Loog Oldham and Led Zep's Peter Grant – Bill Aucoin prospered by the use of one all-important code: '*Imagination sells*'. And with Kiss as the ultimate adolescent dream machine, how could he fail? Inspired profiteering? Callous manipulation of mommy's purse-strings? Regardless of the answer, Kiss were getting seriously rich on the results...

★ By April 1976, having established themselves both as a major musical and business force, the quartet released their first studio album to make serious chart inroads. 'DESTROYER' was produced by Alice Cooper collaborator Bob Ezrin, reached No.11 in the States and became the band's first LP to chart in the UK, hitting No.22 at the end of May on a five-week stay. Sales were undoubtedly helped by their inaugural visit to the UK that same month.

FROM NEW YORK TO ALPHA CENTURI

★ During a four-day stop-over, the group played dates in Manchester's Free Hall and London's Hammersmith Odeon (May 13/14 and 15/16, respectively) and gave thousands of English fans their first opportunity to witness the Kiss experience: Simmons' eerie blood-drooling (a genuinely spooky sight), Frehley's rocket-firing guitars, Stanley's acrobatic stage prowling, Criss' mini-castle of a drum-kit – all were on show. Yet, stripped of the bombast of their more spectacular effects – Kiss were unable to bring their full stage set with them due to the relatively diminutive size of British venues – the overt theatricality of their act seemed somewhat hollow on the small stage, and as result, audiences left venues with a peculiar mixture of elation, confusion and, for some, disappointment.

Ace Frehley earns his nickname 'Mr Excitement'

★ The trip was nevertheless a useful introduction for the band to the home of their musical ancestors, and they took full advantage of the curiosity their presence generated by being heavily photographed at various London landmarks, including the Houses Of Parliament and the Tower Of London. As in the States, they would not allow the press to capture them without make-up or stage costumes. The shows and publicity would result in *Alive!* entering the charts alongside *Destroyer*, with the concert album reaching a semi-reasonable No. 49. Yet any hopes of a US style take-over bid remained grounded for the moment.

★ But what about that new studio album, *Destroyer*? Well, it was 'quite a production', as they say. Indulging their creative side to full effect, *Destroyer* saw the band and producer Bob Ezrin experiment with choral harmonies, orchestration – courtesy of the New York Philharmonic Orchestra – and taped effects, in an effort to push back the boundaries of their sound. The result was the most complete Kiss album to date, with the glorious testament to the

rock star ego 'Do You Love Me' (covered several years later by young British hopefuls Girl, who featured future Def Leppard guitarist Phil Collen in their ranks), Simmons' self-defining 'God Of Thunder' (though it was written by Paul), the head-on collision of 'King Of The Night Time World' and, of course, the sickly, sweet lyrical yearning of 'Beth' all featured. Nevertheless, the standout track on the LP was surely 'Detroit Rock City'. Written by Stanley with producer Ezrin, in homage to the Detroit fans who'd packed the city's Cobo Hall three nights in a row for the band's recording of *Alive!*, the song was a graceful, yet biting rocker, built on the back of powerhouse drums, duelling harmony guitars, and held together by Paul's best vocal.

★ *Destroyer* captured the strange essence of the band like nothing else that had gone before, and contradicted many critics' suggestions that they were little more than musical bubblegum. To celebrate the LP's release on June 15, Casablanca issued their first ever promo record, in the form of a four-track 'Tour Special' featuring the tracks 'Beth', 'Do You Love Me', 'Flaming Youth' and 'Detroit Rock City'. Pushing up the sales of *Destroyer* further by ensuring radio-play, it's now become a valuable collector's item.

★ But *Destroyer* wasn't without its problems, particularly those between Ace Frehley and Bob Ezrin. The guitarist was incensed when the solos he'd recorded for certain tracks were deemed unsuitable by the producer, and on the arrival of top session man Dick Wagner – brought in to tidy things up, particularly on the track 'Sweet Pain' – the usually even-tempered Frehley all but exploded. The decision, ludicrous in consideration of the Space-Ace's undoubted fretboard talents, would sow the first seeds of discontent in his heart, and start him seriously questioning his place in the scheme of the Kiss machine.

★ "Bob didn't have much patience with me," said Ace. "If I didn't have a solo worked out or was having trouble coming up with a melody, he would just bring in someone else, like Knucklehead McGuiness or whatever the fuck his name is. That's when I lost all respect for Bob Ezrin... I don't think he put in enough time with me. He catered to Paul and Gene because they were the songwriters. And I think a producer's job is to work with everyone in the band. I don't dislike him as a person, and I think he's a great producer, but I just don't ever want to work with him again."

★ Despite Frehley's studio misgivings, Kiss hit the road relatively carefree, spending much of the year touring the hell out of the world – starting in Canada, with new costumes designed by Jules Fisher Associates. The new look, debuted in cartoon form on the cover of *Destroyer* saw the band resplendent in metallic black and silver, with the familiar stack-heels spiralling even higher (Gene's boots taking on demonic form, with gargoyles' heads appearing where his toes should have been) and the costumes growing ever tighter. In fact, Paul's was barely able to contain him, the hairs on his chest spilling dangerously out of the spandex! The stage show too was given a major up-lift, with an expanded lighting rig – accompanying the chase lights on the band's logo – and enough smoke-bombs to sink a battleship. Group choreography was also enhanced, the three mobile Kiss members performing increasingly complicated physical manoeuvres to consolidate the stage show's theatrical power. The routines were now so adventurous that Gene, Paul and Ace narrowly avoided doing serious damage to each other, guitar necks missing heads by inches as they shot across the boards.

★ As the *Destroyer* tour rolled into the USA, Kiss received the first in a set of bizarre tributes to them, tributes so strange in the life of a rock'n'roll band, that they beggared belief:

★ For instance, on October 9, the band visited Cadillac High School in Cadillac, Michigan, where the resident football team demonstrated their latest sporting innovation – the 'Kiss Defence' system. Designed by the school's assistant coach, who had written to the group to proclaim the strategy's success on the playing field, Kiss were so intrigued with the story that they took time out of their busy schedule to watch the team in action – even agreeing afterward to perform a concert in the school gym for 2,000 students.

★ A day later, Kiss were rewarded for their kindness by the Mayor of Cadillac and his various officials, who presented the band with the keys to the city. In a scene from *The Outer Limits,* the dignitaries all donned Kiss make-up for the presentation, and then led a parade on the city's main street in the quartet's honour – renamed Kiss Boulevard especially for the day.

★ A month later there was to be another extraordinary date in the Kiss calendar. On November 21, the band flew to Terse Haute, Indiana for the first official gathering of the Kiss Army, on what was termed Kiss Day. The Kiss Army was the fiercely combative name given to the group's fan club, and they could be rather fanatical, as Terse Haute found out.

★ "The Kiss army was a singular and peculiar event," recalls Simmons. "It started in Terse Haute, Indiana. This guy wanted to hear Kiss on a local radio station outside the city. The station refused and said, 'We don't play Kiss'. He said, 'If you don't play Kiss by 5pm, the Kiss Army will surround your station, and you won't be able to leave'. And sure enough, the guy got all his friends, and the place was surrounded."

★ Stanley: "And the next day he sent locusts!"

★ Simmons: "So, we decided: 'Let's call our fans the Kiss Army. They have a real take-no-prisoners attitude'. The Kiss Army is a show in itself and will have a big part in this tour. Mardi Gras has nothing on the Kiss Army. And you better believe the natives are restless."

★ What next? Kiss nuclear warheads, each one painted with a band member's face? Don't laugh...

★ Meanwhile, on July 21, 1976, Casablanca introduced recent Kiss fans to the combo's first three studio albums. *Kiss, Dressed To Kill* and *Hotter Than Hell* were put out as a box set, with a 16-page booklet, six Kiss cards, a Kiss Army sticker and literature on the fan club. Only 250,000 of these were pressed, and they sold out almost instantly.

★ But back with the bizarre, in August, Kiss actually sold kisses – at 93 cents a slurp at a record shop in Atlanta, Georgia. The reason? Charity. Every cent they raised went to the Muscular Dystrophy Campaign. Though spectres of savage self-promotion still swayed in the background, it was good to see the band using their image in a different, more humane manner, and for such a worthy cause.

★ In November 1976, *Destroyer* paid Kiss another dividend when the album's main ballad, Peter Criss' 'Beth', reached No.10 in the US singles chart, becoming their biggest hit to date. A saccharine-coated smoocher telling the tale of the absent drummer's desire to be at home with his girl, the tune almost turned out to be something very different. In fact, when Gene Simmons first heard the lyrics, he thought it was about a man:

★ "(I said) Gee, that's an interesting idea. What's it about? Jeff Beck?"

★ "No man, it's about Becky," replied Peter, referring to his then girl.

★ "You should change that," challenged the wise old demon. "Make it 'Beth', otherwise they're going to think you're pitching for the other team."

★ One hasty re-write later, the song shuffled its way on to *Destroyer.* Eventually 'Beth' became the only tender moment in the Kiss live canon – with Criss singing it sitting on a stool, holding a rose out to the audience. It was a hit largely by default. Released originally as a B-side to 'Detroit Rock City', it was only when radio stations flipped the record and put the ballad on their playlist that the public picked up on its simple, if irritating, charm.

★ That same month, Kiss' eagerly awaited new album

'ROCK AND ROLL OVER' was rush released

to take advantage of the new singles' success. Creating

an immediate stir with its circular, sci-fi inspired sleeve

(check out Ace's laser beam eyes), the LP quickly scaled the

charts, jarring to a halt at an impressive No.11. It would

remain on the *Billboard* Top 100 for 45 weeks.

★ After the exceed-to-succeed policy of *Destroyer*, the band went back to basics for their new disc. Recorded in a disused theatre, the Star in Nanuet, New York, the album featured legendary engineer Eddie Kramer, and the pairing provided some splendid results. Raw, savage and occasionally brutal, *Rock And Roll Over* featured such high-energy workouts as 'I Want You', 'Mr Speed', 'Take Me' and the future show-stopper 'Makin' Love'. Ballsy, no-nonsense anthems sure, but after the intricate subtleties and orchestral experimentation of *Destroyer* it was a welcome return to old ways. And besides, Kiss hadn't abandoned all sense of sonic innovation – with Peter Criss consigned to record his drum parts in the theatre's bathroom for maximum echo (only communicating with his colleagues and producer via closed circuit TV camera), the group were still not afraid of going out on a musical limb. Even if it did mean putting the Cat out.

photo-calls was interpreted as rock star posturing, and Kiss were given the cold shoulder. Ridiculed in the press for their 'less than real' approach (Geoff Barton of music paper *Sounds* being the group's only champion), they retired confused and hurt to America, not to return again for four years. If England couldn't be bothered to understand them, then why waste valuable (and profitable) time turning the tide? The band would have their revenge within a year or so, with the lyrics to *Rockin' In The USA* on *Alive II*. A blow-by-blow account of their travels around the world, every country was given a glowing lyrical reference, bar poor old Blighty: "I went to England too, there wasn't much to do" growled a suitably irritated Gene Simmons. And a nation mourned.

★ Interestingly, the second pressing of the record listed Ace Frehley as assistant producer. Why? Maybe it was Kiss' way of smoothing over his ruffled pride after the arguments with Bob Ezrin on the previous album.

★ *Rock and Roll Over* was rough and ready – a brave move considering their new-found popularity. At least one track from the album sessions, 'Queen For A Day', remains unreleased officially. Chances of the song seeing the light of day some 20 years later remain slim.

★ Consolidating their position as rock monsters at home with the huge sales of their latest effort, Kiss reconsidered the possibility of domination on a global scale. Driven by God-like status Stateside, and with ambitions to expand the empire into European soil, the group decided to return to Great Britain for a promotional visit on the back of *Rock And Roll Over*. Invasion, however, was not on the cards.

★ With the country in the throes of a punk revolution, their refusal to strip off the make-up for interviews and

★ But if the UK had provided Kiss with an unwelcome surprise in its lack of hospitality, it was nothing compared to the one waiting for Ace Frehley as the group toured the USA in support of *Rock And Roll Over*. On December 11, 1976, the guitar player received a surging shock to his system at the Civic Center in Lakeland, Florida. Walking down the brand new lighted stairs Kiss had installed as part of their ever-growing stage set during set-opener 'Detroit Rock City', Frehley wobbled on his stack heels, literally electrifying himself.

★ Ace takes up the story: "Gene ran down the stairs on the first song, and I walked down nice and slow – my balance wasn't so good. The power in the building was weird that night, and when I came down, I was grounded out as soon as I touched the metal railing with my hand. Once I got loose, I just fell back – I was out. I had burns all over my fingers. When Paul realised what had happened, he told the audience I was having a problem(!). They all started chanting my name, and that kind of got me going again. It took me at least ten minutes for me to get back to feeling somewhat normal."

★ The shocks were only just beginning for the Space Ace...

At the beginning of 1977 Kiss learned that *Rock And Roll Over* had been certified platinum in the States. It was the third time they'd hit this milestone, and a celebration was in order. It would come within a month, with the band performing a triumphant homecoming concert at New York's Madison Square Garden on February 18. The venerable and prestigious venue was packed to the rafters, and the gig itself was a real sign of how far the band had come in just a few years.

★ "I used to tell my folks I'd end up there one day, and they'd always laugh," Criss told *The New York Times* the night before the show. "So tomorrow night (when) we're playing the Garden... when I think about that I get cold."

★ To add to Peter's chill-factor, the group's new single, the countrified 'Hard Luck Woman' (sung by the Cat-man himself) hit No. 15 in the US. If that wasn't enough, Kiss' third album *Dressed To Kill* was certified Gold the same month. The first of the three pre-*Alive!* records to reach that mark, it was conclusive proof that fans were eating up anything with the Kiss logo on it. Far beyond just a theatrical phenomenon, they were now an awesome hit machine. As if to seal that status, 'Calling Dr. Love', Simmons' lusty musical cure for all ills, was released as the second single from *Rock And Roll Over* in March. Within weeks it had climbed to No. 16 in the charts. Life had never been so good.

each member of the group donated a vial of his blood to the ink mix of the comic, thereby ensuring every buyer could now own a small part of the Kiss legend. The gimmick worked, with *Kiss – The Comic* selling some 400,000 copies, a Marvel record that would stand for over a decade. Though the idea was copied by other musicians in the future (including Alice Cooper and Aerosmith), no band ever repeated the success of Kiss in the comics medium. With an image ideal for such an experiment, who could have? As Paul Stanley would later say "You didn't see 'Marvel Comics presents The Eagles'!"

★ No, you surely didn't.

★ Three months before the ground-breaking comic hit the street, on March 18, Kiss took off for Japan on what was dubbed at the time the 'Sneak Attack' tour. Playing concerts in four main cities, Osaka, Nagoya, Fukuoka and Tokyo, the band smashed previous attendance records in the country when they made a four-night stand at the famous Budokan Theatre. Topping even The Beatles in terms of bums-on-seats, Kiss' oriental trip created sheer pandemonium in the normally gentile oriental surroundings. Limousines carrying the New Yorkers were almost lifted from the ground by fanatical fans, and various members of

Kiss visit Japan in 1977

★ Historically, an even more significant event was to occur in June 1977, when Marvel Comics – home of such characters as The Uncanny X-Men and the friendly neighbourhood Spider-Man – immortalised Kiss in their very own comic. Capturing the mysterious spectacle of the band in glorious primary colours, Kiss were transformed into superheroes – with the power to fly, shoot gamma-blasts from their eyes, travel effortlessly between dimensions and encounter some pretty nubile women on the way. Suffice to say, they'd saved the world at least once by the end of the story.

★ In an extraordinary marketing ploy to promote sales,

the group were chased through the city streets by love-struck Japanese girls. Still, if rumours are to be believed, Gene Simmons didn't seem to mind at all, preferring instead to be caught by as many as he could! It wasn't just oriental beauties that attracted our Gene, though. In fact, the Kiss bassist's 'stiff propositions' were making quite a name for him with ladies the world over. Long of tongue and horny as hell, Simmons was alleged to have a photographic 'keepsake' of each and every woman he had ever encountered. Single-handedly putting Eastman-Kodak films where they are today, Gene should be congratulated for his friendly and open approach to the female species. After all, he does not draw distinctions based on looks alone: "I pretty much fancy all women. Fat, thin, short, tall, young, old, anything." A true diplomat of the sexes.

PLATINUM BLUES

★ Triumphant, but tired by all the recent activity (especially Gene), Kiss returned home on April 4, 1977. They elected to take a brief vacation – their first real break since *Alive* had shot them into the rock stratosphere. Retiring into the arms of wives, girlfriends and family for some well-deserved rest and relaxation, the leave of absence ended as abruptly as it had begun when, in early May, the painted foursome were re-called to New York's Record Plant Studios with producer Eddie Kramer to begin recording the follow-up to *Rock And Roll Over*.

The real Batman shows off his cape

★ Working quickly to ensure a summer release, even

Kiss must have been awe-struck when on June 30, the new

album `LOVE GUN` was certified platinum on

advance orders alone. One million copies already sold –

and the LP wasn't even in the shops...

★ Again packed with a winning combination of no-nonsense hard-rock battle cries, and sly, sexually charged lyrics, *Love Gun* displayed a band totally in command of their strengths – and more than willing to use them. The title track, written by Stanley on his recent flight to Japan, was a bruising, mid-tempo assault, all humorous chest-beating and frenetic lead-guitar runs. 'I Stole Your Love', a fine companion piece, twisted and turned on arrogant stop/start rhythms and unrestrained vocal gymnastics. Simmons too proved himself in exceptional form with the gritty 'Plaster Caster'. An X-rated tale of his 'experiments' with the Chicago Plaster Casters (a legendary gathering of groupies who encased musicians' genitalia in plaster for posterity's sake), it rattled along like a freight train, stopping only to pick up more double-entendres on the way. But perhaps the biggest surprise of the record was Ace Frehley's singing debut, 'Shock Me'. Destined to become his signature tune, this Stones-inflected stomper was awash with clever chord changes, and screaming, bad-tempered solo-flights. When the extended version of the song hit the concert halls, it allowed the Space-Ace a stunning opportunity for improvisation and unbridled showmanship, his beloved Les Paul oozing smoke and feedback before ascending on hidden wires towards the heavens.

★ *Love Gun* – its title a strange spoof on The Sex Pistols, then making massive waves in Britain – came with a free plastic gun, a cheap yet collectible item for the ever-growing ranks of the Kiss Army. Featuring another painted cover (this time with the band atop a misty platform, adoring females at their feet), the disc also marked the first performance of The Kissettes, three female backing singers brought in to broaden the group's musical palette. However, with the ladies' contributions largely inaudible amongst the Marshall amps, their inclusion remains something of a mystery.

★ This latest in the line of Kiss albums spawned its first hit single in July, when the libidinous 'Christine Sixteen' (its classic line "I don't usually say things like this to girls your age" still unforgettable) hit No. 25 on the US chart. One of the most fondly remembered, if lyrically dodgy, numbers from *Love Gun*, it ended up a Simmons song, only because the Demon beat Stanley to the punch. According to Gene, Paul was planning to write a tune with that title, but the bassist – recognising a classy name when he heard one – immediately began work on a demo version of his own, with a couple of then unknowns in tow: brothers Eddie and Alex Van Halen. When the final version was recorded, Ace apparently copied the future father of modern rock guitar's solo note for note.

★ Warmed up by the success of 'Christine Sixteen', and following a tradition now cast in stone (as well as plaster), Kiss set out on the road in support of *Love Gun* – starting the ball rolling in neighbouring Canada. The new stage set to accompany the tour was a monster of design and their most ambitious yet: hydraulic lifts for musicians and drum-kit rising majestically from the boards to tower above the audience; mammoth pyrotechnics in the form of smoke bombs, confetti storms and fireworks showering the front rows, and enough amplification to deafen a continent. With the added bonus of flame throwers and a huge multi-coloured lighting rig framing the whole spectacle, it was the biggest rock'n'roll circus ever, and the band were justly proud of it.

★ As if to put the proverbial cherry squarely on top, Kiss also unveiled new costumes for the tour – still predominantly in the black and silver theme of their previous incarnations, but now as lavish and over the top as their latest production… Gene was evil personified, resplendent in thigh length metallic boots, and a bat-like leather cape; Paul, ever the lover, in skin-tight ebony, boasted a shaggy, tousled mane that would shame any Shetland Pony. Peter, a wild alley cat, had a studded collar around his neck, and as for Ace, well let's just say his wrap-around silver wings would have flown him to Alpha Centuri and back, no problem at all. It was left to then rising stars Boston pop-rockers Cheap Trick, to act as opening act for this theatrical juggernaut.

★ Unsurprisingly, Kiss never seemed to worry about taking quality support bands out with them. They knew that however good their opener might be, nothing was ever likely to match the bewildering chamber of horrors the headliners had in store. Hollywood mogul Samuel Goldwyn had once said that his ideal film began with a climax and built from there. Kiss had simply taken the idea, and turned it into a career.

★ On August 7, 1977, the *Love Gun* tour steam-rollered across the States, soon installing the group in Los Angeles for a mammoth three-night stand at the city's 20,000 seater Forum Theatre – on August 26, 27 and 28, respectively. Eager to document what was becoming musical history in the making, and undoubtedly monopolise on the proven success of their previous concert LP, the decision was made to record the Forum shows for future release. To add to the general sense of excitement surrounding the dates, Gene managed to set his hair on fire for the seventh time. However, it was unlikely anyone noticed, as massive jets of flame burst forth around the Wild Cat emblazoned drum-riser behind him! And to think, in the early days he only had a seven-pronged candelabra to keep him company…

★ The following month, Kiss received another huge boost when they were over whelmingly voted No.1 band in a Gallup Youth Survey of 1,069 US teens. Additionally in September, the band's stage outfits were installed in the Hollywood Wax Museum. Bela Lugosi, Vincent Price… and now Kiss. Was there no end to it? Well yes, especially if you happened to be a critic or a feminist….

★ Though the teenagers of America had taken Kiss to their collective hearts, others were less impressed with the group's accomplishments. Influential rock magazines such as *Rolling Stone* had largely ignored Kiss for years, seeing their brand of self-marketing savvy and pop-metal bluster as coarse and childish in equal measures. Choosing instead to focus their attentions on more 'credible' acts such as Patti Smith and Bruce Springsteen, the signal the serious music press was sending out was not hard to fathom – 'go away, you're not wanted'.

★ The feminists too, had their doubts. While Kiss may have been seen by many as a celebratory, life-affirming experience, female intellectuals pointed an accusing finger at the lyrics, stating that they carried appalling examples of

misogyny and deviant sexual practice to the nation's youth. The quartet were quick to defend themselves, pronouncing women sacred creatures for whom they had much respect. However, with titles like 'Love 'Em, Leave 'Em' and 'Two Timer', and lyrical phrases such as "When I saw you coming out of school that day, that day I knew I gotta have you" blotting their song-book, the activists may have had a valid point.

★ The greatest anti-Kiss lobby, however, came from various religious sects dotted around the USA, which saw the group as sinful, white-faced demons sent to Earth to cause chaos and anarchy. The fact that Kiss were just four reasonably well-adjusted New York boys who'd stumbled on a God-given gimmick didn't seem to matter a jot. To the God-fearing folk of Biblesville, USA, they were the spawn of Satan, and the records had to be burned. Kiss largely ignored the accusations, taking solace in the fact that you had to buy the records before you torched them! Still, the fanaticism must have shaken the group a little, as the number of body-guards around them continued to rise at an impressive rate. Such strangeness. You can be sure it never happened to The Partridge Family.

★ As if to spite their detractors, nearly two years after

Alive had broken Kiss wide open, its much-anticipated

follow-up – imaginatively titled **'ALIVE II'** arrived

on the heels of the group's latest concert tour. It was to be

their masterpiece.

Gene Simmons breathing fire
on stage circa 1977

★ The result of the recent Forum shows took up three sides of the release, the band showcasing their best numbers from *Destroyer, Love Gun* and *Rock And Roll Over* to devastating effect. Opening with the manic announcement "You wanted the best, and you got the best, the hottest band in the world – KIIIISSSSS!!!!", 'Detroit Rock City' roared out of the stereo and into your living room in a frenzy of deafening explosions and over-driven guitars. Backed up with 'King Of The Night Time World', 'Ladies Room' and the nuclear assault of 'Makin' Love', when *Love Gun*'s brutal riffing closed side one you knew there was nowhere to hide.
★ Sides two and three only added to the party. Continuing the almost impossible energy level, 'Calling Dr. Love', 'Christine Sixteen' and Ace Frehley's apocalyptic 'Shock Me' (replete with extended soloing and howling interplanetary feedback) all shot by in a sonic flash, before the Nashville swing of 'Hard Luck Woman' finally brought temperatures down for the first time. Nevertheless, the respite was only temporary as 'Tomorrow And Tonight' again picked up the tempo, and led to a bone-crunching 'I Stole Your Love'. Peter Criss' gentle 'Beth' was next up, giving romantics everywhere a breather before Gene Simmons' flame-shooting, blood-spilling 'God Of Thunder' proved he really did gargle with lighter fuel. In the end, it was left to Paul Stanley to whip up a vocal fire-storm on 'I Want You', before the curtains finally fell on a rousing 'Shout It Out Loud'. In over 55 minutes of earth-shattering noise, the crowd had not once stopped screaming...
★ The three sides of music captured on *Alive II* would come to personify the Kiss experience for all time; wild,

good time rock 'n' roll, soaked in atmosphere and heavy on celebration. With lashings of audience participation and little or no regard for introspection or pseudo-intellectual posturing, this was simply the sound of 20,004 people having some serious fun. And almost twenty years later, they still sound like they're enjoying themselves.
★ The fourth side of the album was a departure from the concert hall, taken up instead with new studio material cut with Eddie Kramer at the Capital Theatre. Featuring the songs 'All American Man', 'Rockin' In The USA', 'Larger Than Life', 'Rocket Ride' and 'Anyway You Want It', Kiss showed a more aggressive edge to their nature here, with a wired, rasping sound to the guitars previously absent on other releases. The reason? Ace Frehley had gone A.W.O.L.
★ Only showing up at the sessions to record his own psychedelic stomper, 'Rocket Ride', before pulling an unexplained vanishing act, Kiss were left with little alternative but to draft in old friends Bob Kulick and Rick Derringer to complete lead guitar duties on the remaining studio tracks. Displaying the first *real* signs of an unpredictability that would soon become commonplace, the Space-Ace was obviously more interested in surfing the stars than flying around the fretboard that week.
★ Nonetheless, it allowed fans the luxury of hearing what Kiss might have sounded like, had they chosen Bob Kulick over Frehley at their guitar auditions all those years ago. The moustachioed session player had run a close second to Ace at the time, and from the sound of the squealing, moody leads present on 'Larger Than Life', it was easy to understand why. In another universe, perhaps...
★ Whatever demons may have been plaguing Ace Frehley were quickly exorcised though, as he re-joined the group in November for tour duties to promote the new LP. Starting their latest leg of concerts mid-month at the Myriad Convention Centre in Oklahoma City, Kiss finally hit home on December 14, 15, 16, when they performed three sold out shows at Madison Square Garden. Total attendance: 60,000.
★ As if to top it all, in December, Kiss were crowned the second highest selling artists of the year in America by industry magazine *Billboard*. What's more, they were the only act that year to have three platinum albums certified to their name. Merry Christmas, indeed.
★ In January 1978, Kiss released another single in the States, this time a live version of 'Shout It Out Loud'. Yet when it only reached No. 54 – their lowest placing since 'Rock And Roll All Nite' had stalled at No. 68 in May 1975 – critics were quick to signal the end of the Kiss era.
★ Despite this temporary setback, the band would steam ahead, making an appearance at the American Music Awards via satellite from Largo, MD. They performed 'Rock And Roll All Nite' – *quelle* surprise. Kiss obviously appealed to television in 1978, as chat show host Edwin Newman also employed their services, interviewing them on his top-rated US TV special, *The Land Of Hype And Glory*. Presenting themselves as witty, articulate and intelligent, their appearance must have surprised many who thought all rock bands to be mono-syllabic and self-obsessed.

★ On February 2 1978, the domestic run of the
Alive II tour at last ground to a halt with two sold-out
shows in Providence, Rhode Island. But that wasn't the end
of the story by any means – there were still a lot of jewels
left on that new live album, and the group were going to
plunder them. The same month, 'Rocket Ride', the first Kiss
single to feature Ace Frehley on lead vocals (and the only
one to ever feature the legendary lines "C'mon, grab a
hold of my rocket"), was released to stores. True to form,
the single quickly hit the Top 40.

★ Seemingly inexhaustible, Kiss capped it all by
playing a record five sold-out shows back in Tokyo's
Budokan Theatre (March 29 – April 2), eclipsing the
four-night record set by The Beatles and... themselves.
It was a tremendous finale to a quite legendary tour.
But how could the band hope to ever top it? Well, how
about making a movie?

★ Before we enter the world of film production though,

there was the compilation album of remastered tracks

called  Released in

April 1978, and promoted by group and record company as

a celebration of Kiss' hallowed status, it was in reality yet

another collection of previously available material, similar

in content to both *Alive* and the extremely recent *Alive II*.

A worthy testament to a pop phenomenon, or a cynical,

money-grabbing marketing exercise? You decide. Still, the

record lived up to its name, and gave the band a much

needed breather from further recording and touring for the

time being. After all, they needed it. They were about to

become movie stars.

★ During May and June, Kiss spent five weeks filming
Kiss Meets The Phantom Of The Park at Magic Mountain
in Valencia, California, incorporating a free live show on
May 19 to be used in the movie. Unfortunately what had
appeared on paper as a promising *Star Wars* type fantasy,
turned out instead to be a tacky, Z-level bore, drawing on
tried and tested horror/sci-fi themes for its inspiration.
Set in a theme park run by a mad scientist (played with
maximum ham by Anthony Zerba), the plot – such as it
was – saw our evil Einstein trying to replace the real Kiss
with evil androids for his own nefarious purposes.
But with the group possessing super powers (and in Ace's
case a wicked sense of humour), it wasn't long before
evil was vanquished, and the world was set to rights on the
back of a song.

★ Yet, if Kiss' first cinematic experience was hardly up
there with *The Godfather*, it did serve instead as a telling
indicator of behind the scenes cracks in the band's armour.
Peter Criss, bored by the latest in a string of gimmicks,
was showing all the discomforting signs of cabin fever,
deliberately missing cues and refusing to show up for voice
dubbing after initial filming had been completed. It was
left to an unknown actor to dub his vocal contributions.

★ Ace Frehley, similarly challenged with Gene and
Paul's newly found thespian leanings, often arrived late on
set (hung-over from the night before), and like Peter,
showed little interest in post-filming duties. Fragile egos?
Chemical 'problems'? Or warning signs of real dissension in
the ranks? Time would tell.

★ After completing the picture, the band found
themselves still in the fantasy world, as Marvel Comics
(flushed by the unprecedented success of their first Kiss
special) tried to repeat the dose. On August 28, the industry
giant shipped the second Kiss comic book to stores,
and yes, it proved again to be a best-seller, falling just shy
of *Kiss – The Comic*'s previous success.

★ Rock-stars or super-heroes? It was becoming an
uneasy question, especially to Ace Frehley who would later
voice his concerns of the time: "I didn't agree with all the
merchandising – the lunch box, the cards, the dolls, etc.
I didn't want us to become a teeny-bopper group, and
all that merchandising was putting us in that category.
I think it turned off a lot of our hard-core fans – the fans
that used to come see us in small clubs, when we were just
a small, kick-ass rock'n'roll band."

★ But if Frehley was harbouring doubts about
the Kiss machine, he was soon to be coaxed out of his
questioning by the next move on the band's surreal agenda:
solo albums.

★ On September 18, 1978 four separate LPs bearing
the trademark Kiss logo were released simultaneously to
a waiting world. Each bore a bold painting of the relevant
group-member in full make-up, their name subtly
placed in the right-hand corner of the sleeve. Without
doubt, these solo discs were Kiss' most ambitious move yet.
No band had tried the experiment before them, and
certainly none has done since. Yet, was the idea another
in an increasingly long line of clever gimmicks, or genuine
artistic endeavour? And, most importantly, were the
records any good?

with the transition . Not even the pleasant, insistent danceability of 'You Matter to Me' and 'That's The Kind Of Sugar Papa Likes' could turn their opinion around, and the LP soon stopped selling. An all-round disappointment, it was obvious to all concerned that, 'Beth' aside, people preferred the cat when he had his claws out .

★ A Hollywood-style extravaganza, Gene Simmons' solo effort `GENE SIMMONS´ displayed his sense of humour and diversity to remarkable effect, ping-ponging from the raunch and lust of 'Radioactive' and 'See You In Your Dreams' (a corking re-work of the *Rock And Roll Over* original), to the inspired acoustic balladry of 'See You Tonite' and 'Always Near You/Nowhere To Hide'. Gene even managed to find time to honour his childhood hero, Lon Chaney, with the moving 'Man Of A Thousand Faces' – a tune originally written in 1970 when Simmons was still part of garage band Bullfrog Bheer. Never boring, and suffused throughout with the spirit of The Beatles (the Demon King's favourite band), the record was an unexpected surprise, even going so far as to end with a cover of Jiminy Cricket's 'When You Wish Upon A Star' that stayed remarkably close to its source in both tone and feeling. Gene called on the services of many celebrity friends for his effort – including Bob Seger, Aerosmith guitarist

Gene Simmons gets acquainted with his microphone

★ Easily the most musically accomplished and accessible of the four, Paul Stanley's solo effort was a stylish and feisty collection of tunes, more sophisticated perhaps than the singer/guitarist's day job, but losing none of the grit listeners had come to expect of him. In fact, numbers such as 'Wouldn't You Like To Know Me' established Stanley as the true heart of the band in many eyes, and his ability to float between romance – 'Hold Me, Touch Me' – and rock – 'Move On' – illustrated effectively where Kiss gained much of their two-tiered approach. A mature and assured recording, employing the services of such established industry veterans as drummer Carmine Appice and Bob *Alive II* Kulick to add extra class, `PAUL STANLEY´ ensured that should the Star-Child ever wish to leave the Kiss bubble, he had a fine start on his CV.

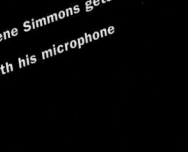

★ Ace Frehley, to no-one's surprise, offered a walk on the wild side. If 'Paul Stanley' was the heart of Kiss, then

'ACE FREHLEY'

was surely its soul. Full of hard rock idiosyncrasies such as the venomous 'Rip It Out', the stoned 'Ozone' and the killer 'Wiped Out' – "I was wiped out, I had my lights out" – the Spaceman's solo outing was a hugely enjoyable slice of gonzoid dynamics, with only the haunting instrumental 'Fractured Mirror' allowing us to see the more gentle side of the man. Produced by Eddie Kramer, and powered along by the drum vitriol of buddy Anton Fig, the guitarist's solo outing seemed little concerned with commercial success. Yet, Frehley had a hidden card up his sleeve in the form of Russ Ballard's 'New York Groove'. When launched as a single, this catchy and likeable salute to his hometown proved a surprise hit, reaching No.13 in the US charts on December 2. It just goes to show, you never can tell. Legend has it that Frehley recorded most of the record whilst flat on his back in the studio. If that's the case, then more people should follow his example.

★ However, as good or bad as the albums might have been, the general response from the public, in sales terms, must have really wobbled the group. With Gene Simmons' effort flying highest at a disappointing No.22 – followed by Ace, Paul, and Peter at Nos.26, 40, and 43, respectively, this was not the usual fanfare accorded to Kiss product – more a ritual snubbing. Had they finally overstretched themselves?

★ It certainly appeared time for a re-think, not least for the American music industry officials who compiled the charts. Despite the solo LPs' poor sales showing, all four had still been accorded platinum status. Reason? Gold and platinum certification was based on shipping figures to shops, and not real over-the-counter sales. In an overhaul of the process, compilers introduced the now standard practice of certifying million sellers on *actual* units shifted, rather than advance orders, or albums distributed. Altogether a fairer, more honest system, but a real kick in the teeth to the Kiss marketing team. Critics retired to their beds warm at night...

★ The real motive for the solo albums' release would eventually emerge years later – mollifying Ace Frehley and

Peter Criss. Growing tired of the never-ending round of tours, records and increasingly bizarre promotional chores, the guitarist and drummer were threatening to jack in their jobs in favour of other more recreational pursuits. Simmons and Stanley, fearful of losing what they had worked so hard to achieve, suggested the stand-alone projects as a compromise – a way of cooling the jets until the old enthusiasm returned. Sanity prevailed, and Ace and Peter agreed to the idea.

★ In truth, the whole vainglorious exercise might never have seen the light of day if Kiss hadn't been signed to the most outrageous record company in America. Many saw Casablanca's indulgence of their No.1 asset's latest whim as a cave-in to rock-star ego, and surely a step too far – even for them. "(Neil Bogart) pressed so many that we were getting killed on the returns," moaned one former executive of the company. Still, what doesn't kill you makes you stronger...

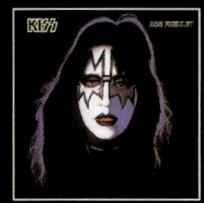

Ace Frehley's 1978 solo album

'Love Gun' live

★ Remaining defiant, the band ploughed on, re-establishing old heights on October 28, when NBC premiered *Kiss Meets The Phantom Of The Park*. Achieving the TV company's second highest viewer rating in 1978, with only James Clavell's sprawling epic *Shogun* topping it, the movie at last pulled off the trick of taking Kiss into nearly every home in the USA. Not at all bad for four dodgy thespians appearing in what can best be described as a waste of ninety minutes.

★ Ultimately, to add to the numerous honours bestowed on Kiss in their salad year (and at last take away the sour taste of those solo LPs), Gene Simmons' satanic stage outfit was borrowed by the United States Smithsonian Institute for a world-wide exhibit called 'American Art' in November. Featuring designs for such icons as Elvis Presley and Cher (Gene must have been familiar with this one), the travelling exposition's wish to use Kiss costumery illustrated that the band was now not only a musical force, but an endemic part of Americana as well. From rock'n'roll wannabes to cultural institutions in less than a decade, the Kiss phenomenon seemed truly unstoppable by the time the snow began to fall.

Facing Page:
The Demon King and friend

After a prolonged Christmas break, Kiss returned to active duty in February 1979, beginning work on their first studio album in nearly two years. Enlisting the services of Vini Poncia (the producer behind Peter Criss' solo LP), the result `DYNASTY` was a step further away from their hard-rock roots, but a cracking little effort nonetheless, brim-full of memorable tunes and sophisticated songwriting.

★ Relying on the commercially-astute Poncia to illuminate the way, *Dynasty* was the first Kiss LP to really sit up and take notice of what was going on in the outside world. The lead-off track, 'I Was Made For Loving You' (co-written by Stanley, Poncia and the then-unknown Desmond Child), typified the new approach. Bowing its head to the disco craze sweeping through America at the time, the song rattled along like Chic-on-heat, with falsetto vocal interludes, popping bass fills and a shuffling, danceable beat. Quite unlike anything the group had attempted before, it was a quantum leap from the hardware displayed on *Rock And Roll Over* and *Love Gun*.
★ Elsewhere, tunes such as the silky 'Sure Know Something', the bitter-sweet 'Magic Touch' and the funky 'Dirty Livin'' consolidated the sonic cultivation, presenting listeners with a polished elegance few had thought possible of Kiss.
★ It wasn't all sweetness and light. The raucous Rolling Stones cover '2,000 Man' and the arrogant 'Charisma' still stung in all the right places, and Frehley's auto-biographical 'Hard Times' left no doubt that the Astronaut, at least, had not lost sight of his less salubrious origins: "We had to fight to be accepted, it wasn't

Paul Stanley proudly displays his valet skills

right and I protested. For hanging out, we got arrested, everyday life in the city..."
★ Ace may have been a multi-millionaire, but his head was still firmly planted in the Bronx.
★ A pot-pourri of dance, raunch and lissom charm, *Dynasty* was all things to all people, its only fault perhaps the diversity of its grooves. Still, that didn't seem to matter to America's record-buying public who, warmed up by the massive singles success of 'I Was Made For Lovin' You', pushed the LP all the way up to No. 9 in the charts – making it a triple-platinum hit. Legitimate as well!
★ But if Kiss appeared on the face of it to be enjoying this latest bout of glory, the behind-the-scenes picture was far from rosy. Peter Criss, at the point of *Dynasty*'s triumph, was a loose cannon waiting to go off. In the midst of a growing love affair with booze, and increasingly given to emotional tantrums, the drummer only showed up for four out of the nine tracks on the record, leaving Simmons, Stanley and Frehley in a musical no man's land. With zero alternative, the band turned to Anton Fig – the percussive thunder behind Ace Frehley's solo outing – and Richie Fontana, a seasoned sessioneer, to complete the disc. Bored, listless and reluctant to tour, Criss was confronted by Gene about his attitude and was alleged to have said: "I'm gonna sell ten million records myself. I don't need to be in a band." Mmmm... The whole sorry state of affairs was heart-rendingly captured in the band's own *X-Treme Close-Up* video documentary, where Simmons was filmed on the *Dynasty* tour, leading Peter out of the dressing room and onto the stage by his hand. The look of despair on the Cat-Man's face has to be seen to be believed.
★ Still, from the cosy picture of the four on the sleeve of *Dynasty*, and the pounding sounds contained inside, you'd never have known there was trouble brewing at mill.
★ Somehow pulling the seams together, Kiss began their American tour in support of the LP on June 15, in Lakeland, Florida. With the inevitable brand new staging – sleek white ramps engulfing stadium boards – and fresh costumes – Gene and Ace were big on shoulder pads that year – the show was a combination of old glories and current material. It also incorporated songs from the band's solo projects. Gene was let loose on his pop-rocking 'Radioactive', Paul on the Stones-influence swagger of 'Move On', but the best of the bunch was undoubtedly Ace's infectious 'New York Groove'. Donning a staggering chase-light guitar for the tune, Frehley literally lit up the house. Hokey? Las Vegas for adolescents? You better believe it, but the effect was nothing short of magic.
★ The day after the *Dynasty* tour opened, Kiss were handed a very early Christmas present, as 'I Was Made For Lovin' You' became a certified hit. Crashing into the charts at No. 11 on June 16, it spent another several weeks circling the *Billboard* Top 30, before acquiring gold status in July. The song was also the first single from the band to make an impact in Britain, reaching a respectable No. 50. Its mix of chugging Les Pauls and Giorgiou Moroder beat may have confused older fans, but 'I Was Made For Lovin' You' was doing a splendid job of introducing Kiss to a hitherto untapped market – a market which had never even considered them seriously before.

BETTER THAN DALLAS?

★ As their latest tour rolled on, the group received another boost to their popularity as the top-rated cable TV channel HBO premiered a *Kiss Concert Special*. Only real superstars got this sort of treatment from television stations in the pre-MTV days, and Kiss took full advantage of the boon, by handing in a stonking performance for transmission.

★ Keeping up the momentum, another single was pulled from *Dynasty* in September – the velvety smooth 'Sure Know Something'. Blessed with a lilting, almost hesitant vocal from Paul, and several changes of mood and pace, the song seemed a sure-fire hit. Unfortunately, it couldn't match its predecessor's gallant success, and stalled at a disappointing No.47 in the US charts. Back to the drawing board.

★ A month later, Kiss consolidated their latest campaign with Gene and Ace's appearance on radio's *Budweiser Presents The Robert Klein Hour* – again a very prestigious occasion. During the taped segment, Klein asked Simmons if his legendary tongue could reach the bridge of his nose. In typically sardonic mood, Simmons memorably replied: "It can reach the 59th Street Bridge."

★ This wasn't the first time Gene's prominent protuberance had attracted attention. Rumours had circulated since the early Seventies that the Bat-Boy's tongue was in fact that of a cow's, transplanted into his head for 'satanic' reasons. Another apocryphal tale had the bassist putting it to use in a New York bordello for the pleasure of whomever happened to come along. It was just as well nobody picked up on the story of Peter Criss' adventures with another, more elegant, tongue at the *Hotter Than Hell* photo sessions all those years before. Suffice to say, the model who attended the shoot certainly had a soft spot for our Peter. Have another look at that sleeve for the

evidence – Feline or fellatio? Whatever the case, Criss looks over the moon with all the attention he's getting...

★ By the end of the Seventies, magazines all over the world were clamouring to get a shot of Kiss without their make-up. Several existed of course, but the mutually beneficial relationship the band enjoyed with photographers had precluded them from being published. Until November 1979, that is. A chubbier-than-usual Paul Stanley was captured leaving the famed Studio 54 night-club in New York City, and within hours his face – *sans* black star and flaming red lips – was all over the tabloids. Would this intrusion destroy the mystique so carefully built up over a period of years? Not quite yet, but it did call into question just how long Kiss could keep up the disguise. Glam was long gone – replaced instead with new-wave and dance music – and the band were starting to appear faintly ludicrous against the skinny black ties and drain-pipe jeans modelled by hot acts like The Cars and Blondie.

★ Nevertheless, Gene Simmons thought the war paint should stay, likening the idea of removing it to Father Christmas discarding his togs: "There's nothing worse than Santa Claus coming out (of the chimney) and saying 'Oh, by the way, you're feeling great about this – well, it's all fake. Let me take off my red suit – see the pillows underneath? I'm really your Dad. It would ruin the magic."

★ The make-up stayed. At least, for the present.

★ In December 1979, as Santa set out to calm any fires Simmons' remarks may have fuelled, Avco Embassy Pictures finally released *Kiss Meets The Phantom Of The Park* to cinemas worldwide – giving starved fans from Paris to Plymouth the opportunity to see their heroes in action. Perhaps, in consideration of the movie's dubious quality, they were better off staying at home.

★ Yet thespian credibility was far from Kiss' minds, as their return tour finally ground to a halt on December 16. After a group lay off of nearly two years, personnel problems in the studio and growing concerns as to whether they could still hack it in a music world dominated by sneering young pretenders, the band had returned with one of their biggest albums yet. Around the corner, things were about to get rocky.

1979: On tour in support of the three million selling 'Dynasty'
Facing Page:
Classic Kiss – (Left to right):
Ace Frehley, Paul Stanley, Peter Criss & Gene Simmons

Dynasty's commercial success had served Kiss well. Giving them a strong foot-hold from which to enter the new decade, the record had also secured the group an all-important new audience with the cleverly crafted dance-pop of 'I Was Made For Lovin' You.' Keen to monopolise on their good fortune, it came as no real surprise that when they re-convened at New York's Record Plant Studios in February 1980 to begin work on a follow-up, their choice of producer remained Vini Poncia. Imbuing the band with a lighter, yet still steely touch on the three million selling *Dynasty*, Poncia was considered just the right man to evolve their sound to even greater heights. Well, that was the theory.

★ First, however, there were certain other matters to deal with, including the persistent rumours circulating in the press that Peter Criss was no longer part of Kiss. At first, denials were issued followed by a wall of stony silence. But after an anxious two months of waiting, fans finally got to hear the verdict.

★ On March 16, in a blaze of attendant publicity, it was officially announced that Peter Criss was indeed leaving the band to pursue a solo career. The split, according to both parties, was entirely amicable and no ill-will was involved. Peter would soon be releasing details of his new solo project and Kiss, for their part, would seek a replacement for their dearly-departed moggy in due course.

★ The truth was somewhat different. Criss had all but given up on Kiss in the last eighteen months and despite Gene and Paul's entreaties to him to reconsider his position, he would not be moved. Agreeing to have his image appear on the album cover for contractual purposes only, Peter's last act in Kiss as a fully paid up member would be to film a promotional video with the group for the up-coming single, 'Shandi'. Then, he was free. Criss had been with Kiss seven years.

★ Sources eager to belittle the drummer put the blame for his exit on escalating drink and drug problems. Others say Peter harboured resentment towards what he saw as the controlling faction of Simmons and Stanley. Surely the pressure of being in the Kiss bubble 24 hours a day, 365 days a year must also have taken its toll. After all, when asked in 1975 to sum up how he perceived his newly acquired celebrity status, Criss' answer hinted clearly at a psyche ill-prepared for the future rocket ride: "It's funny. I don't feel like a star, and I think that maybe that's good – because if I did, I might go crazy."

Kiss mark two – Eric Carr (second from left) joins Kiss in 1980

★ In the end, to Kiss circa 1981, the reasons for Peter's departure were irrelevant – the cat was out of the bag and there was an album to finish.

★ Wanting to put the whole affair behind them as quickly as possible, the three remaining members re-doubled their efforts, and with the assistance of Anton Fig, again filling in for Criss, had their latest record mixed and ready to fly by June. The result of their endeavours `UNMASKED` was undoubtedly the worst record Kiss ever made. Relinquishing their gutsy roots in favour of an all-out pop attack, the LP was as tasty as a half-cooked biriyani. Tunes such as 'She's So European' and 'Tomorrow' died almost before they had begun, choking in a mix of syrupy vocals and neutered guitars, and with the appalling 'Shandi', the group surely stooped to an all-time low. Insipid, irritating and bereft of any real emotion, the song smacked of calculated radio-friendliness – a deliberate and merciless attempt at producing a hit. Only Frehley's humorous 'Torpedo Girl', Gene's 'Naked City' (co-written with Bob Kulick, amongst others) and a cover of Gerald McMahon's acid 'Is That You' came anywhere near Kiss' former power. Make no mistake, *Unmasked* was dreadful.

ALL THE KING'S HORSES

★ Arriving in shops in a cartoon cover, telling the tale of a photographer's fight to get a shot of the band without make-up (the punchline: when 'Unmasked', Kiss' real faces are the same as their disguises), the album provided Kiss with their worst seller in five years. Falling well short of the usual platinum status, *Unmasked* reached only a disappointing No.35 and No.48 in the US and British charts, respectively, and its failure sent out a clear signal to all concerned that their reign as rock's crown princes was over.

★ Perhaps it was the loss of Criss that had finally unravelled the magic. After all, Kiss had built themselves publicly on an 'all for one, one for all' attitude, and with the drummer's departure, that illusion had been destroyed. On the other hand, it might have been the fans' feeling of betrayal at Kiss' dereliction of hard-rock duty. In reality, it was very probably the fact that Kiss had released a terrible LP, and the punters – quite rightly – had refused to buy it. The band themselves didn't have time to dwell on the reasons though, as they were hard at work finding a replacement for Criss.

★ Kiss, in fact, had started the process of auditioning new drummers on May 17 – before *Unmasked* had come out – but with over 2,000 applicants to see, it was well into June before the list had been narrowed down to a possible ten. Peter Criss, in the friendliest of gestures, acted in an advisory capacity to the band, and checked out the many contenders to his throne. It soon became clear as daylight to all that one man was head and shoulders above the competition: Eric Carr.

★ Born on July 20, 1950, and a native New Yorker like Gene, Paul and Ace, Carr tore through his final audition with all the power of a bull elephant. Impressing Kiss with his confident takes on such numbers as 'Strutter', 'Firehouse', 'Is That You?' and 'Black Diamond' (during which he also showed his prowess as a vocalist), there was no doubt that when Carr at last put down his sticks after an electrifying 'Detroit Rock City', he was their boy. Diminutive in stature sure, but Carr had a God-given ability to hit drums like a heavyweight pro, and Kiss wanted it. Eric graciously accepted the band's invitation to join.

★ The guys had already decided that whoever got the job shouldn't be asked to take over Peter Criss' make-up. It would have been discourteous to both Criss and his fans, and it would put the new recruit in a difficult and embarrassing position right from the off. Nonetheless, the war-paint was still an essential part of the group's theme, so Paul, Gene and Ace had taken it upon themselves to design a hawk-like visage in anticipation of their next member. Impressed with their handiwork, they were sure Eric would love it.

★ He didn't. Even though he had only been with the band a matter of days, Carr rejected the bird-image full-on. He had something else in mind – a fox. Thankful their new drummer hadn't proposed a duck or worse still an ostrich, Kiss went with it. And so it was, that when Eric Carr was fully introduced to media and fans at the Palladium in New York on July 25, he was a wily dog, instead of a cunning hawk. The result? An ecstatic response from

the Kiss Army, who welcomed the drummer to their ranks with open arms. Carr returned the compliment with his inaugural speech: "I love being in this band. It's like a dream come true for me. To be playing with these guys is just awesome."

★ Kiss' new member was already very much a part of the organisation when the group returned to the UK and Europe in August 1980 for their first ever real tour of the territories. Supported by English band Girl, Kiss played the biggest indoor arenas available to them – including Stafford's Bingley Hall and a triumphant two-night stop-over at London's Wembley Arena on September 8/9. It was clear to everyone who attended that Gene, Paul and Ace had found a monstrous replacement for Peter Criss. Bringing himself up on a staple diet of Led Zeppelin's John Bonham, Eric re-energised old material such as 'Love Gun' and 'God Of Thunder', and brought violent authority to newer songs like 'Is That You?' Loud, assured and brimming with strength, Carr lit a candle under Kiss' collective posterior.

★ Freed from the restrictions of the smaller stages they had played before, the band gave English audiences their first glimpse of the full-on Kiss attack. Bathing the crowd in white light, fire-bombs exploded, confetti storms raged and smoke-pots engulfed the front rows. One fan – who'd been lucky enough to get close to the band at Wembley Arena – got blood splattered all over his left hand by Simmons at the height of The Demon's oral convulsions. So overawed was he by the experience, that the lad refused to wash his mitt for two whole weeks. The crown may have slipped on the record-front, but Kiss still knew how to give a party.

★ While the band were touring Europe, they received a much-needed boost to their popularity at home when they appeared on the cover of America's huge-selling *People* magazine on August 8 . The accompanying feature included lengthy articles on all four members, including Carr, and pictures of Simmons' celebrity girlfriends, Diana Ross and Cher. The biggest shock, though, had to be the publication of the first official pictures of Kiss without their make-up. Two years previously, such a move would have been unthinkable, yet there it was, in glorious technicolour. It was the beginning of the end of an era.

"When you wish upon a star..."

★ As their world-wide trek wore on, the band next found themselves setting sail for a five-week stadium tour of Australia on November 9. Performing a total of 11 sold-out shows with attendance figures between 40,000-70,000 per night, the heavy profit margins involved helped to make the whole *Unmasked* outing Kiss' most profitable jaunt to date. It also aided the air-brushing of drastically falling record sales. There was little doubt that they were on the wane, but with the lucrative overseas market still eager to embrace them live, the quartet could postpone a financial drought almost indefinitely. It was a timely reminder of their business acumen. Like the Romans, Kiss knew when it

wasn't going well within the city walls the easiest way to re-establish power was to invade another country.

★ At last, on December 3, 1980, the last date of the *Unmasked* campaign was played out at Western Springs Arena in Auckland, New Zealand. When Kiss reviewed their extremely busy year, it read like this: lost one drummer, found another one; released a critically lambasted and commercially disappointing album to domestic audience; wowed the rest of the world live. What was next? A break certainly, but after that there was the unenviable task of winning back America. As the boys retreated for the winter, they knew 1981 would only bring more hard work.

★ Understanding the burden Kiss faced, and keen to give the group some breathing space before tackling that next crucial LP, Casablanca Records fired off a hastily assembled 'Best Of The Solo Albums' release in January 1981. A disjointed and jarring affair, the disc only served to illustrate just how far apart the four Kiss members' musical tastes were. If the group were to go forward with new drummer Eric Carr, they would have to pool their efforts instead of further diversifying them.

★ On March 1, the group re-united at Ace Frehley's Ice In The Hole Studios – built at his house in Connecticut – to begin work on their new album, ostensibly titled *Rockin' With The Boys*. Buoyant from the news that *Alive* had been submitted to the US Library Of Congress as one of only 800 examples of the finest American music (your guess is as good as mine), spirits were high, and sessions were expected to go well. Yet, within weeks, a collective decision was made to abandon the project in favour of a radical change in direction. The material recorded, such as the excellent 'Deadly Weapons', was to be shelved indefinitely.

★ Precisely what triggered the switch in tactics is still uncertain. The songs that Kiss had been working on were in the *Unmasked* vein, and in consideration of the response accorded that album, it may have been felt that a further dalliance with pop would have done them irreparable damage. It could also have been a reaction to accusations concerning their three-chord approach. After all, critics had enjoyed a field day for years with the simplicity of Kiss songs, and while the slurs concerning their musical ability were largely untrue – Simmons was a fine, melodic bass-player, and Frehley a spirited, unusual soloist – they may finally have had enough of the bitching, and wanted to fight back. Maybe it was just a moment of madness but whatever the reason, the band took over New York's IRS Studios in May to tackle their first ever concept album. The man brought in to oversee recording was old friend / enemy Bob Ezrin. Ace Frehley must have been thrilled.

★ When it became clear that IRS was unsuitable for the sound they were looking for, Kiss upped sticks to the Record Plant, just around the corner. But when the sessions there failed too, the whole ensemble decided to fly to Toronto to give Bob Ezrin's home studio (known as Ezrin Farms) a try. Gelling in the new climate, Kiss spent a further three months refining what they had, and at last ceased work in September 1981. The five months the project had taken was a record for the band. When asked by the press and fans what to expect, Kiss remained cagey, taking an attitude of 'Just wait and see...'

'(MUSIC FROM) THE ELDER' was unveiled to all. A strange and complex record and a huge migration from the group's standard sound, it flitted between out and out heavy metal – 'Dark Light' and 'I' – to gentle ballads like the lilting splendour of 'World Without Heroes'.

The LP's schizophrenia was nowhere better summed up than on 'Mr Blackwell'. Hazy and compelling, swirling in and out of a mist of melody and grind, it was either a work of inspired genius or pretentious twaddle, depending on your point of view.

★ As for the concept behind the album, well, that was just as difficult to work out. Essentially a tale of a secret society of elders charged with the responsibility of Earth's well-being against the forces of evil, the story confused as much as it enlightened, leaving listeners wishing they had taken esoteric studies at school.

★ Unlike anything before it, *(Music From) The Elder* even managed to divide the hard-line Kiss army in two. But not casual fans of the band, it has to be said. They knew exactly where they stood on Kiss' latest experiment: An equal distance between apathy and aversion. *(Music From) The Elder* peaked at an appalling No.75 on the US charts, failing to even generate 500,000 sales.

★ It was obvious to all that Kiss had shot themselves in the foot with this one. Having re-defined their sound on *Dynasty*, they then diluted it completely with *Unmasked* – a concept album that swung alarmingly between gentle introspection and clattering histrionics was just one step too far for the average music buff. Had they elected to return to the hard-rock bombast of *Rock And Roll Over* or the challenging themes of *Destroyer*, things might have been different but, as it was, they had little alternative but to take their latest disappointment like men. Eric Carr must have wondered just what he'd bought into.

★ On November 22, Kiss tried to reverse the tide with the release of the wistful 'A World Without Heroes' as a single. A moody, contemplative ballad with some seriously eccentric chord changes, the tune restored some honour when it ascended to No.56 on the *Billboard* charts, but overall the damage was already done. Taking the hint, the band neglected to tour on the back of the LP, and aside from a televised appearance on ABC's *Fridays* show in the States (where they performed 'The Oath', 'A World Without Heroes' and 'I') and a live satellite broadcast to the San Remo Music Festival in Italy, they soon retreated into the shadows to lick their wounds.

★ *(Music From) The Elder* had done Kiss irreparable harm. Not only had it alienated much of their remaining audience after the atrocities of *Unmasked*, it had left them stranded between musical posts. What were they now? Rock? Pop? Progressive? Or worse still, finished? A blinding return to form was needed if Kiss were to survive. But they'd have to do it without Ace Frehley.

Gene Simmons holds his legendary 'Axe' bass

Early into 1982, Kiss announced the somewhat distressing news that their not-so-secret weapon, the inimitable Ace Frehley, was to leave the group. As with the departure of Peter Criss, the decision was amicable, and Ace would be sticking around long enough to give a hand with their new album. So, what had caused the latest defection? And, most importantly, did he jump or was he pushed?

★ Well, by all accounts, Ace Frehley had been a fully paid up member of the Lost In Space fan club long before the confirmation that he was to leave the band. Unpredictable by nature, and making up his own rules as he went along, in truth, the guitarist had spent much of the Seventies and thus far all of the Eighties in an semi-alcoholic haze.

★ Frequent drinking bouts with friends and band staff had been par for the course (Frehley couldn't share his enthusiasm for the bottle with Gene and Paul as neither imbibed), and at times they'd seriously affected his ability to contribute to the Kiss canon. That wasn't to say, though, that the results weren't sometimes funny. Take for instance, the band's appearance on the *Tom Snyder* TV Show in the Seventies: it was meant to be a semi-serious exchange of views, with Kiss allowing themselves only an occasional witticism at the expense of their genial host. Yet, from the start of the interview, it was obvious to anyone watching that Frehley was loaded, and incapable of taking anything seriously. Therefore when Snyder, plainly ignorant of rock'n'roll terminology, asked Gene Simmons if he is the bass (pronouncing it as in the fish) player, Frehley lost the plot and cackled uncontrollably. "Yeah, and I play the pike." It took the narrowing of Gene's eyebrows to restore the guitarist's control...

★ However, it wasn't just Ace's bouts with the bottle that were causing Kiss concerns. He seemed also to have lost interest in even playing with the group. A glaring example of Kiss' dilemma had occurred only months before at their contribution to Italy's San Remo Festival, when Frehley hadn't even bothered to show up. Gene takes up the story:

★ "Ace was in The Twilight Zone. We did an Italian festival with the biggest stars in the world in '81, where 600 million people watched on a satellite feed from Studio 54. We did it as a trio. Why didn't Ace show up? He was at home watching a ball game. 'Ah, you guys do it, what's the big deal?'"

★ It wasn't as if this was the first time either. Kiss had been making excuses for their resident astronaut's extra-curricular voyages for ages. Check out this random selection:

★ "He's not around as much these days. He's got a wife (Jeanette) and kid these days and for a while they've been his priority." – Paul Stanley, on why Frehley didn't hang around with the rest of the band on tour.

★ "We've been together for about 10 years and there's a certain amount of flexibility you have to have because of the people that you care about. So the fact that Ace has to deal with certain domestic things that are important to his lifestyle is something you understand and live with. He's married, we're not." – Simmons on Ace's domestic bliss.

★ "When Peter Criss was having his ups and downs physically we went and had other drummers line up just to make sure we could fulfil our obligations and it's the same thing with Ace. We've committed ourselves to 100 dates, which is the first part of the tour. Everyone's got personal problems. I like to, I don't know, bang my head against a wall, and sometimes some of us like to do other things, but we don't want to feel that because of one person we may not be able to complete the tour." – Stanley (on the rumour that Kiss had secretly been auditioning guitarists to replace Frehley).

★ "Ace will be with us, but we might have another guitarist at the side of the stage to supplement the sound. He wouldn't be a member of the band and wear make-up, just a sideman." – Eric Carr on Ace's future stage role.

★ Whether Frehley knew Kiss were coming to the end of their tether with him remains a matter of conjecture, but he assures us now it was his decision to leave, and not a sacking. According to Ace, the making of *(Music From) The Elder* had a lot to do with it:

★ "That album really was the icing on the cake, as far as me leaving the band is concerned. For starters, they brought in Bob Ezrin to produce, who I (didn't) relate to that well. Plus I felt that the music... wasn't where we should have been going at that point. I felt we should have done a real raw, heavy album instead of a slick, bullshit concept album. When I heard the final mix, I didn't even want it released – but I was outvoted. They cut out half of my guitar solos without telling me – and I had done some amazing stuff. I remember taking the cassette and smashing it against the wall. And it was our least successful record. So I know my gut reaction was right."

★ Kiss lost more than just a guitarist when Ace handed in his cards. They'd also lost a valuable songwriter. Giving the group some of their best moments with the likes of 'Cold Gin', 'Parasite', 'Hard Times' and 'Strange Ways', he had additionally been responsible for the best of the band's solo albums. Seen as 'the real deal' by many of Kiss' fans, 'Mr. Excitement' (a term used by those around him to describe his laconic personality) was not going to be easy to replace. Few guitar players fire rockets while they play.

LEAVING EARTH ORBIT

★ Shorn of Frehley's wayward genius, the band nevertheless began recording a new EP (tentatively titled 'Severe Cuts') at the Los Angeles Record Plant studios in March. Understanding the need to move quickly lest rot set in for good, four songs were worked on: 'Nowhere To Run' (originally composed at the *The Elder* sessions) 'Partners In said Paul. "But what makes it worthwhile for us are the four new songs which are pretty indicative of what Kiss is about right now."

★ Gene too, sounded out the band's reasoning behind their latest move: "We talked about an EP, a single and all that. But we finally decided on the *Killers* format because in a lot of countries some of the catalogue isn't out or isn't permanent, and also because there's a new audience out there who may not be familiar with the history."

Crime', 'Down On Your Knees' and 'I'm A Legend Tonight'. To aid them, Kiss turned to old friend Bob Kulick for some of that searing guitar he'd brought to the fourth side of *Alive II*. Yet, as with the *Rockin' With The Boys* project that had preceded *The Elder* some months before, the band changed their minds and shelved plans to release the material on an EP. The tunes would eventually turn up on yet another compilation album 'KILLERS' in May.

★ Nonetheless, unlike recent experiments, the songs Kiss had produced this time were a fine return to their older values. Tough as anything that had graced *Rock And Roll Over* or *Hotter Than Hell*, but retaining that important commercial edge, they proved that the group could still cut the hard-rock mustard, with or without Frehley. Paul, on lead vocals for all four tracks, was in especially fine form. Proud of their efforts, Stanley and Simmons faced the press on *Killer's* release:

★ "Our label wanted something to hold everybody until the next studio album. I don't think at this point we're huge fans of compilation albums, 'cos we've had enough of 'em,"

★ The biggest boon of the project had to have been the pairing of Kiss with a new producer, Michael James Jackson. Unlike Vini Poncia or Bob Ezrin, Jackson seemed to understand instinctively what the group were about, and his ability to capture their sound at full-throttle boded well for the future. *Killers,* with Ace Frehley's face on the cover despite his lack of involvement, was their first record in ages to actually sound like... Kiss.

★ Gene and Paul, warmed by the album's positive reception, showed no hesitation in re-joining Jackson as co-producers of their next full effort in July 1982. Returning to LA's Record Plant Studios, with the ebullient Eric Carr in tow, the trio employed an equal number of guitarists to replace Ace Frehley on their latest undertaking: sessioneer Steve Ferris, future jazz/blues maestro Robben Ford and a certain Vincent Cusano, otherwise known as Vinnie Vincent.

★ After three months in the studio, the word was out that Kiss had a monster on their hands. To demonstrate the seriousness with which they were taking it, the band even turned down an approach to appear at the Monsters Of Rock Festival at Castle Donington in England during August in order to continue their work. Simmons, however, did take time out to explain what was coming our way: "This album is meant to tell everyone there's to be no more fooling around, no more artistic self-panderings, and that's in no way apologising for anything we've done because we're really proud of *The Elder*. But this is right between the eyes. This album will be even harder than *Rock 'N' Roll Over*. This is Metal 'N' Roll in certain respects. The heaviest album we've done yet."

world to hear what had made them so confident.

'CREATURES OF THE NIGHT' was a classic.

Taking Led Zeppelin as their blue-print, the group blew away the cobwebs that had tangled them up on *Unmasked* and *(Music From) The Elder*, and showed anyone willing to listen that they were still a force to be reckoned with. Beginning with the awesome thunder of Eric Carr's drums (superbly captured throughout by Jackson) the LP's title track glistened with energy, driven along by a superb Stanley vocal and Steve Ferris' scatter-shot riffing. Followed closely by the menacing 'Killer' (a track Gene had co-written with Vinnie Vincent), the next highlight arrived in the shape of the salty 'Keep Me Comin'. A not-so-subtle tribute to Led Zep in general and Jimmy Page in particular, its insistent groove mixed the chorus of 'Whole Lotta Love' with the inspired soloing of 'Ramble On'. Derivative yes, but still a corker. Sweeping through 'Rock And Roll Hell' and the energetic 'Danger', the record then produced its greatest moment with 'I Love It Loud'. An ear-shattering mix of stop/start rhythms and brutal guitar abuse, this Simmons/Vincent anthem in the making single-handedly crucified any cynics who thought Kiss were only good for the scrap-heap. Taking down the pace with the reflective power-ballad 'I Still Love You' and muted 'Saints and Sinners', the record's finale returned the sonic thuggery of 'I Love It Loud' to make its point. 'War Machine', with its bone-splitting riff, and throaty Simmons growl ended *Creatures Of The Night* with a bang.

★ Though it was the best thing the band had produced since *Alive II*, it still did not do the trick of restoring Kiss to their former seat of power. Despite good reviews (for a change), and an overwhelmingly positive response from the remaining hard-core fans, the damage done in recent years meant that the band had to content itself with No.45 in the American charts. It was a blow for the band, who had bust a nut creating it, but 30 positions better than their last record had fared. Nonetheless, *Creatures* did reasonable business in Europe, with England giving it a semi-impressive No.34 placing in the Top 50 when it was released there in April 1983. Any talk though, of a second coming would have to wait. Still, the fighting spirit was back: "We wanna get hungry again," said the Rocky Balboa-like Simmons. "I think that at a certain point we became a bit remote... we've got to get in touch with what made us in the first place."

★ Unfortunately, the making of *Creatures Of The Night* had been touched with tragedy. Neil Bogart, Casablanca Record's leading light, and the man who was instrumental in building Kiss' profile all those years ago, died from cancer before the album had been released. Bogart, extremely close to his charges and displaying considerable faith in them throughout their career, would have been as proud of *Creatures* as they were, and Kiss felt his loss greatly. As a mark of remembrance, the LP was dedicated to his name.

Vinnie Vincent (centre) replaces Ace Frehley in 1983

★ Itching to get back on the road and show off their new wares, Kiss still had the problem of officially replacing the errant Ace Frehley. Even though the Space Ace had been erroneously credited as contributing to their latest offering, the world and his wife knew he was long gone, and were rightly eager to know who was going to fill his shoes. The answer was Vinnie Vincent.

★ Blessed with emotion and frightening technique, Vincent had also co-written three of the finer moments on *Creatures*. Hungry, confident and on the face of it well balanced, he was the obvious choice. Gene, Paul and Eric

Kiss mark three captured offstage

★ "I was born Vincent Cusano in Brooklyn in 1952," he told them. "I started banging away on the guitar when I was three or four years old, but it wasn't until the early Sixties that I got seriously involved, took lessons and developed an interest in the classical side of music, which I really love. I took a job in a department store burning old boxes during the late Sixties, but most of the time I gave guitar lessons to earn a living. I got my big break when I moved out from New York to LA at the start of the Eighties.

★ "I met Adam Mitchell, who co-wrote three of the songs on the *Creatures Of The Night* album and we began to work together. Then Adam did some writing with Gene and I said, 'I'm gonna meet this guy if it kills me'. I had nothing to lose, so one day I saw him sitting there, and went over and gave him my phone number and asked him to call me if he wanted to co-write with someone else. I swear to god, I went home and waited by the phone for a week straight, not sleeping or eating. Finally, Gene called and the first songs we came up with were 'Killer' and 'Shout It Out Loud'. I was so excited I was literally going out of my mind.

Then Gene introduced me to Paul and we ended up writing 'I Still Love You' and a couple of other songs.

★ "When auditions were being held to find a replacement for Ace, I must have made the biggest pest of myself and probably the biggest fool, too. I just nagged Gene constantly. I told him, 'I know I'm right for this band, just give me a chance, give me a shot. I'm gonna kick this band's ass!' Then, one day I was taking a bath when the phone rang. It was Gene, offering me the job. I tell him I'll phone him back, then get out of the bath and start screaming like a lunatic. I'm running from room to room, standing in corners and banging my head against the wall. This must have gone on for 20 minutes until, finally, I managed to compose myself and call back. Gene said, 'Take a flight to New York and we'll rehearse. We've got a tour starting...'."

★ Vincent's moment of truth arrived when he took to the stage with Kiss on December 28, in Bismark, USA, for the start of the group's first domestic outing in three years. The crowd's reaction? No problem, you'll do just fine. Vinnie might have been replacing an institution in Ace Frehley, but with a formidable array of trills, slurs, hammer-ons and wild tremolo bombing at his fretboard disposal, he shouldn't have been that worried: "I figured the kids would boo and shout 'We want Ace'," said Vincent at the time. "But they've really accepted me. They send me gifts and fan mail and I'd like to say thank you, because their support is everything to me. Being in Kiss enables me to live out my fantasies both as a guitar player and rock star."

★ Choosing the Egyptian Ankh as his facial symbol within the band, the gold paint that covered Vincent's features may have made him look eerily like a certain astronaut from a distance, but the screams escaping from his Flying-V said otherwise. Kiss had chosen well, it seemed.

★ To coincide with the live dates, the band released 'I Love It Loud' as a single. Things looked good for the song. It was going down a treat in concert, and when *Billboard* recommended it in their 'Top Singles Picks', it seemed Kiss might finally have the hit they needed to bring them back from the brink. Yet the tune only managed a limp No. 102 on the charts. Why? Well, it might well have had something to do with the accompanying video. Featuring bug-eyed teens walking zombie-like into the abyss, the promo caused so much controversy when it was broadcast on TV that Gene and Paul actually ended up having to appear on the CBS show *Nightwatch* to defend themselves against accusations of Satanic worship. The religious protests that had dogged them in the Seventies were obviously far from over.

★ Knights in Satan's service' or not, Kiss soldiered on with the *Creatures* tour for several more months, before bringing the whole thing to a staggering finale at the world's largest arena, the Maracana Stadium in Rio de Janeiro, Brazil, on June 18/19/20, 1983. The group, performed to a total of 247,000 people, smashing their previous attendance records into little pieces.

★ Playing a blistering set that reached its climax with Eric Carr's newly designed 'tank' drum-kit firing smoke bombs into the crowd, Kiss knew that they had come to the pinnacle of their live career. Whatever they did next couldn't possibly top this. Or could it?

★ Plans were hatched to pull off another awesome party in neighbouring Argentina for August, but the concerts were halted by an extremist organisation called The Free Fatherland Nationalist Commando Movement. Threatening to halt the proposed assembly "even if it goes so far as to cost the lives of that unfortunate band", Kiss had no alternative but to beat a hasty retreat home. Any hopes of Gene serenading 300,000 people with an emotive 'Don't Cry For Me, Argentina' died there and then...

★ It was not the first time that Kiss had hit trouble abroad. In Germany, their trademark twin lightning-bolt logo (created by Ace or Paul, depending on who you believe) was deemed to be too close to the infamous emblem of the notorious Waffen SS, Hitler's not-so-secret police. Therefore the group were forced to change the symbol for all future German releases, a situation that continues to this day. No one seemed to care that three Kiss men were actually Jewish!

★ With the latest tour over, and Vinnie Vincent firmly ensconced in their ranks, Kiss had a little time to take stock of their current position. Though remaining a huge concert draw, *Creatures Of The Night* had failed to resolve an embarrassing decline in fortunes on the domestic front,

The four faces on the cover *were* unmasked. Indeed, the only way you could have known it was them was by spotting a huge tongue popping out of the hairy one's mouth...

★ In washing away the warpaint, Kiss created a massive publicity wave that rivalled anything they had achieved in the Seventies. Appearing *au natural* on an MTV special to promote the album, cheekily titled `LICK IT UP' their naked features were soon a talking point for every teenager in America. So shocking was the event, the group even made prime time TV's evening news. Kiss explained the decision to come clean to anyone who would listen:

1983 and the make-up comes off
Left to right: Eric Carr,
Vinnie Vincent, Paul Stanley &
Gene Simmons

and the band were desperate to turn the situation around. The idea of another pop release was out of the question – their remaining audience wouldn't stomach it – and there was nowhere left to go with the live shows. The Rio gigs had been the biggest they had ever done, and to top them would have involved hiring a small country for the occasion. No, if Kiss were to move forward and recapture those bygone glories, they needed a genuine surprise.

★ Wrestling with the dilemma, the quartet reunited with producer Michael James Jackson at Right Track Studios in New York to start work on another album. Deciding to stick with the hard-rock rumble created on *Creatures...,* work went quickly (two months), and the LP was ready for release by September 18. But when it arrived in shops nationwide, it provided fans with their greatest shock yet.

★ "Why have we decided now to take off the make-up?" said the newly naked Simmons. "Probably because everyone has stopped telling us to do it. From the very first day that we came on stage, everyone, including the record companies, has been saying, 'It's ridiculous. get rid of the make-up'. This year, though, they kept quiet, so we figured it's a good time to do it. Also, every single year we see so many bands taking a piece of us – either studs or leather or heels – and we're proud of it. Ten years ago when John Denver was No.1 it wasn't popular to do that stuff.

★ "Everybody accused us of being dinosaurs," continued the bassist, "and they were right – we were the biggest and the baddest, we chewed 'em up and spat 'em out. We did it because we were nuts and we're still nuts. but now that it's become in vogue to wear leather and studs, we wanted to do something different. We want to be out there at the front, though we'll still look like Kiss. If we walk down the

★ Paul later added to his partner's comments, explaining it had been no over-night decision: "We should have taken the make-up off before we did. Some of the guys were a little scared. I tried to get everybody to do it for the *Creatures Of The Night* album," said the former Star-Child. "Just because I thought we were in that grey area between feeling comfortable and believing in that look, and being ready to take the shot and try to go forward. I thought *Creatures...* was a tremendously powerful, focused album. It would have been the perfect time, but the feeling wasn't unanimous, so we waited one more album."

★ Despite the fuss, *Lick It Up* wasn't much cop at all. Lacking *Creatures'* brutal intensity, it limped along on a mixture of cod-metal and steely pop. Loud in all the right places but distinctly absent in soul, only the anthemic title track and the stop/go raunch of 'All Hell's Breaking Loose' could truly call themselves Kiss-worthy. It was a real disappointment after the drama of the facial strip, and the band were again at an uncomfortable cross-roads. Drastic measures were in order.

★ "Kiss has always made its own rules," said Eric Carr, on the defensive. "It did it in the beginning by putting on the make-up and the platform boots and through the stage show, and now we're just making more of our own rules."

★ Making the rules obviously worked for Kiss. Whatever its shortcomings, *Lick It Up* gave the group their best chart placing in America since *Dynasty* in 1980. Climbing to a very respectable No.24, it granted Kiss a reprieve from the 'Where are they now?' club, and a solid footing from which to tour. The clean-up also seemed to work wonders in England, where *Lick It Up* crashed into the Top 10 at a startling No.7. Now that those American chaps had stopped looking so bloody silly, their more conservative cousins from across the water could finally admit to liking them.

★ And finally, what did those ex-members, Peter Criss and Ace Frehley, make of the latest Kiss *coup d'état*? Peter was as elusive as the cat he had portrayed. Despite having released two solo albums since leaving the act (1980's *Out Of Control* and 1982's *Let Me Rock You* – neither troubled the charts), Criss had kept a curiously low public profile and his opinion was confined to a few well chosen whispers. Probably very wise. Ace, on the other hand, was keeping quiet for different reasons. He was still recovering from injuries sustained in a car crash some months before. Driving his beloved DeLorean sports car at over 100mph against traffic on the Bronx River Parkway in New York, Frehley had met with an un-friendly wall. Asked by Pantera guitarist Dime-Bag Darrell some years later if he was loaded while behind the wheel, The Space-Ace's reply was as ever, honest: "(Loaded?) I was beyond loaded."

★ Having moved from the fading Casablanca Records to the more secure Mercury organisation, Kiss began gearing up for a tour in support of *Lick It Up*. Asked by the media whether they were worried how fans would take the new image, Gene Simmons summed up the group's general feeling: "This is a marriage. We're married to our fans, but we're not slaves to them – and they're not slaves to us. We respect their opinions, but you have to act on your own judgement. We're still committed to high energy rock'n'roll and the shows, by and large, will stay the same."

★ So, on October 11, Kiss kicked off their latest jaunt with a six-week sojourn to Europe, choosing sunny Lisbon, Portugal as their first stop. Unfortunately, though the dates went well, they masked a growing problem behind the scenes with Vinnie Vincent. As Kiss returned to the USA for the second leg of the tour, it transpired that the guitar player had actually been sacked while abroad, and then asked to re-join to complete the remaining American dates. What was going on? Paul Stanley kept a dignified silence for the time being, preferring instead to defend the band against jibes that more youthful, aggressive acts were stealing their thunder. His defence was one in the eye for the critics: "What one should remember is that the moon can eclipse the sun, but the sun is always bigger and the moon soon moves away. We don't feel the need to compete with anyone else. Our track record is so unique and overwhelming that to concern ourselves with who's big this year is ridiculous."

Unmasking for MTV in 1983

★ Despite the tough words, Kiss knew they were in a precarious position. Having just achieved a modest rebirth, the only way to meet the challenge of the young lions was through hard work and self-discipline. If you weren't with the plan, then step aside. Vinnie Vincent would do just that on the concluding date of the 'Lick It Up' concert trail in Evansville, Indiana.

★ The date was March 17, 1984. The tour over, Paul could now speak his mind: "He was fired. There's no nice way to put it. It just didn't feel good. There were problems all over the place with him, personal and musical. What's most important to us is that the band runs smoothly and that we deliver the goods 100 per cent. If things start to go rocky and we feel there's a weakness somewhere, then it's time to change something.

★ "Over 20 albums we've had quite a few co-writers and it's no coincidence that every album sounds like a Kiss album. It's also no coincidence that my songs always sound like my songs and Gene's songs always sound like his. I enjoy writing with different people, but I don't necessarily consider what I do to be co-writing. I just like to throw out ideas and have them thrown back to me. So, I won't miss Vinnie as a songwriter at all."

★ Vincent, though, felt he had played his part in the rejuvenation of Kiss' career, and was keen to counter Stanley's opinion: "My chemistry with the band helped put them back on top and gave them a musical credibility that they never had before. Yet I couldn't get the recognition I needed – I felt like I was imprisoned in a small cubicle, like it was someone else's house."

★ As usual with the Kiss camp, generalities replaced specifics when it came to stating exactly why members left or were fired, but Gene Simmons did proffer the following opinion of the wayward axe-slinger in the group's *X-Treme Close Up* video: "The most self-destructive person I've ever met. This guy would hang himself as somebody's offering him the keys to the kingdom."

★ By removing the make-up, Kiss had played the last ace in their pack (Frehley or otherwise). In the war to re-establish themselves fully they would now have to rely on their music alone to do the talking. However, the first problem to overcome was replacing the errant Vinnie Vincent. The answer to their prayers came surprisingly quickly in the form of Mark Norton. A seasoned session man with a formidable reputation for 'lickety-spit' guitar wizardry, Norton came highly recommended to the band. Liking his approach, and impressed with his undoubted command of the fretboard, Kiss were quick to ask him to sign up. There was though, one adjustment to be made: The name Mark Norton sounded a little too ordinary an appellation for a Kiss guitarist. How about Mark... St. John? With all those dollar signs flashing before his eyes, it's unlikely that the latest addition to the Kiss ranks would have objected to Mark St. Slaphead. So, one name-change later, Norton became a Saint, and Kiss had their new member.

★ With 'time waits for no-one' as their motto, the group entered New York's Right Track Studios on July 1, 1984 to begin work on the follow-up to *Lick It Up*. But in a first for Kiss, Gene Simmons was actually absent for some of the recording. Fulfilling a childhood ambition, he had secured his first real movie role as a villain in the Tom Selleck starring sci-fi thriller *Runaway* – and that meant travelling to Vancouver for filming while the album was being made. With Simmons only available for bass duties on four of the tracks, it was left to ex-Plasmatics bassist Jean Beauvoir and Paul Stanley to connect the remaining musical dots. Though seen by the band at the time as a novel distraction for Gene from the world of rock'n'roll, Simmons' new found fascination for all things Hollywood would soon

Paul Stanley with friend and co-writer Jean Beauvoir

blossom into a nagging irritation for Kiss throughout much of the Eighties.

★ Work completed, the latest album from the Kiss production line was released on September 13. Entitled 'ANIMALIZE' an alternative name for the LP might have been *Treading Water*. Consolidating *Lick It Up*'s metal-by-numbers approach, *Animalize* was a safe, anodyne affair, carried along largely on the back of two cracking songs – 'Heaven's On Fire' and 'Thrills In The Night'. Both storming, anthemic rockers in the old Kiss tradition, the tracks seethed and raged while others cowered and fled. Sure, the bone-splintering musical thuggery of 'I've Had Enough (Into The Fire)' and the frenetic charge of 'Under The Gun' showed signs of life, but you knew they were nothing but filler material in comparison to this winning one-two combination.

★ It wasn't all bad though. Paul Stanley, in his new role as producer, had captured the stürm and drang of the Kiss sound well, and Mark St. John's hi-tech twiddlings ensured the band were not lagging behind in the 'watch my fingers fry' school of Eighties guitar, but the overall feeling remained that they could have done considerably better.

★ In the end, no-one seemed to care what caused *Animalize*'s lack of 'oomph' – they were too busy buying it. Crashing into the charts at No.19 in the States and No.11 in the UK, the album provided Kiss not only with what was eventually to be their best seller of the decade (over two million units shifted) but also a genuine sign from the record-buying public that their indulgences of the early Eighties had been all but forgiven. They were back with... well, if not with a bang, then definitely a loud pop. It was time for a celebratory tour.

★ Picking England as their starting point, Kiss kicked off the *Animalize* jaunt in sunny Brighton, England on September 30, 1984. However, any hopes that British fans might have had for being the first to see new recruit Mark St. John treading the boards were soon dashed when it was announced that the guitarist would not be performing on the tour. A temporary replacement, Bruce Kulick, would be covering his duties instead, while Mark recovered from a rather mysterious wrist strain. You could almost hear Ace Frehley cackling from the Bronx... Nonetheless, Kulick acquitted himself admirably and Kiss headed home for the American leg of the tour after a barnstorming set of European shows.

★ Two weeks into the domestic concerts, on November 28, Mark St. John did at last make his début with Kiss at the Poughkeepsie Civic Center, New York. He even managed to put in an appearance at the Broome Convention Centre, Binghampton the following night. But that, as they say, was it. News slowly filtered out that the latest addition to Kiss ranks was to leave after only a matter of months as a result of Reiter's Syndrome, a severe condition affecting the joints of the upper arm. Each time St. John indulged in a spot of soloing, his hands would swell up to twice their size, and the more Mark tried those lightning fast runs of his, the worse it got. What was seen at first as an annoying but temporary strain was now something altogether more serious. Gene, Paul and Eric, to give them their due, tried to find several solutions to Mark's dilemma, even going as far as having his contributions 'shadowed' by Bruce Kulick offstage, but it all came to nought. He had to go.

★ Years later, Gene Simmons would liken St. John's playing to the buzzing of a bee, implying that technique and not soul had been at the heart of his attack. And it's fair to say that Mark St. John was a technocrat, seemingly more concerned with classical arpeggios than ballsy blues scales. But in trying to achieve warp-speed on the guitar neck, he'd actually managed to accomplish the complete opposite: Deadlock.

★ With 19 cities yet to level on their US excursion, Kiss couldn't afford the luxury of breaking for auditions to replace St. John. Besides, in stand-in Bruce Kulick, not only had they a musician who was familiar with their set, but who loved the songs they played. Whether he would take on the mantle of new guitarist could be decided at the end of the jaunt, not now. Without further ado, they again set off on the concert trail, accompanied by the latest addition to their up-dated stage design – a 25-foot-high lighting truss, on which the band could run around above the audience's heads – and support act Queensryche in tow.

★ While Kiss were proving their miraculous powers of levitation at Portland's County Civic Center on November 30, a make-up free Ace Frehley was returning from space just a few hundred miles away. Débuting his new act, Frehley's Comet, at New York's S.I.R Studios to a sell out crowd, the guitarist's voyage home was being touted generally as a second coming. With old friend Anton Fig behind the drums and a mixture of old favourites like 'Shock Me' and fresh material such as 'The Hurt Is On' and 'I Got The Touch' on show, success seemed just around the corner. Record companies, however, disagreed. Seeing Ace as an unknown commodity outside of the Kiss machine, they were reluctant to offer a deal. Destined to roam in the wilderness for another two years, Frehley would eventually find a home for his otherworldly talents at Megaforce World-wide Recordings in 1987. So much for the power of trading on past glories.

★ Nonetheless, if his former colleagues were happy to see the return of the Space-Ace, they didn't have time to show it. Continuing to rock the mid-west for another month, Kiss finally downed tools on 30 December with an explosive performance at Milwaukee's Mecca Theatre. On the international road since September, the band had worked hard at monopolising on *Animalize*'s impressive chart form,

and must have been looking forward to a much-deserved lay-off before resuming tour activities early in the new year. They also had a lot to consider. Though no official word had been issued concerning Mark St. John's problems, it was clear he would not be part of Kiss' future plans. His replacement, Bruce Kulick, was fitting in well with the group's sound, and by his willingness to get stuck in at short notice, he had shown the resilience Paul and Gene were after. It had long been a standing joke between old band friend Bob Kulick and the New Yorkers that his baby brother would be perfect for the band, and Bruce certainly had the instrumental chops. In fact, they had even gone so far as to test them on the last album, where Kulick had contributed the solo to 'Lonely Is The Hunter'. Yet, in consideration of the troubles they had had with the last two incumbents, a trial period was surely the sensible choice. Yes, Bruce Kulick was knocking at the Kiss door sure enough, but they'd only let him in if he knew the password.

1985 brings Kiss mark four (Left to right): Gene, Eric, Paul and new arrival guitarist Bruce Kulick

Bruce Kulick hits the stage in 1985

Kiss started 1985 by releasing a single, 'Thrills In The Night', on January 9. Recommended by *Billboard* as one to watch, it was hoped that the song would crack the Top 50, following on from 'Heaven's On Fire' four months before. Unfortunately, this time Kiss were not so lucky, as the record failed to chart. Nevertheless, the group were easily consoled as, soon after, MTV broadcast their *Animalize – Live Uncensored* long-form video into the homes of a million American teenagers.

★ Attentive to the importance of Music Television in capturing the minds and pockets of under 21s, Kiss were keen to develop a mutually beneficial relationship with the channel. They had, after all, used it as the forum to officially 'unmask' in 1983 – thereby giving MTV a viewer-boosting scoop – and were now simply calling in the favour with the broadcasting of their latest concert show. By continuing to provide the network with a series of colourful, youth-orientated promos throughout the Eighties, Kiss could keep their hand in with this critical adolescent market, and help the video jockeys fill their time-slots to boot. The shrewd business men of the mid-Seventies had found a new and profitable outlet for their unique talents.

★ As the final leg of the *Animalize* tour sprinted to the finish line, Gene Simmons was already renewing his acquaintance with Hollywood. Having dipped a toe into the film world with his portrayal of evil Charles Luther in the futuristic thriller *Runaway* (blowing Kirstie Alley's brains out with a wicked "Bye, bye baby" sneer) the former Devil Incarnate wanted nothing more than to capitalise on the waves his big screen debut had created. Even though the picture wasn't released until December, advance word on Simmons' malevolent, scenery-chewing performance was hot, and offers of more parts were mounting steadily. Choosing to diversify his appeal, Gene would next be seen in the Robert (Freddy Krueger) Englund starrer *Never Too Young To Die*. Playing the part of Ragnar,

a salty hermaphrodite, Simmons sported a gold corset, stockings, and shaved chest. Needless to say, he walked away with the plaudits.

★ "I would play any role in a film, even a gay old-age pensioner," claimed Gene, when quizzed about his daring choice. "I don't care at all about keeping up an attractive public facade. Whatever I was on stage with Kiss could never be classically defined as attractive, but shit, there were certainly enough girls who wanted to fuck that thing. Still, I would love to play some attractive roles as well."

★ Not quite yet. There was, however, a much-coveted role opposite marvellous Rutger Hauer (the eerie serial killer of cult classic *The Hitcher*) in the action packed *Wanted Dead Or Alive*. Again a bad guy, Gene this time starred as an vicious Arab terrorist, destined to die a memorable death as a hand-grenade exploded in his mouth.

★ If losing his head wasn't enough to give him nightmares, then playing DJ Norman 'The Nuke' Tauroc alongside Ozzy 'I'll bite anything, me' Osbourne's twisted preacher in the rock horror film *Trick Or Treat* should have. The only decent actor in the whole sorry shebang, Simmons' stint in the movie did conclusively prove one thing: with his dark, expressive looks and gentle, yet menacing voice he was a cinematic natural, and had a second career in Tinseltown should he wish to take it. But would the bassist really chuck in his day job with Kiss for a life on celluloid?

★ In retrospect, his partner-in-crime Paul Stanley must have had his doubts. After all, Gene had always had a thing for the glamour. Whether it was those not-so-private relationships with singer/actresses Cher and Diana Ross, or the overt theatricality of his days as the Demon King of the Kiss stage, Simmons had enjoyed his life in the spotlight. He seemed to feed on it. Surely this latest opportunity to see his features plastered 20 feet high across a movie screen would prove too much of a temptation to resist?

★ Paul Stanley was the soul of discretion, publicly supporting Gene's thespian leanings while continuing to hold his band together behind-the-scenes. Paul had come too far for too long to let a few feet of film get to him. In the end, it all came right. Gene would continue to take the occasional part during the Eighties, his last appearance in this particular stint being a spot on HBO's uncanny series *The Hitchhiker*, starring opposite Sandra Bernhard in an episode titled *O.D. Feelin'* – but after that, he turned his attentions back to rock 'n' roll.

★ Meanwhile, back in Kissland, a New York high school student called David Lemancke was adding his own particular mark to the group's legend. Obviously bored by the constraints of his art class, Lemancke took it upon himself to paint a 40-foot mural of his favourite band (yes, Kiss) on his school's main wall. None too pleased with the tribute, officials demanded that the homage be removed – double quick. However, the reactionary decree outraged David's fellow classmates so much that they fought back by staging a 50-strong sit-in within the school's main auditorium. While the spirit of rock 'n' roll may have been served, the principal still ordered the janitors to paint over the work. Final score: Crusty old git 1, David Lemancke 0. God bless him for trying anyway.

Facing Page:
"Who's hidden the harmonica?"

HERE COMETH THE POODLES

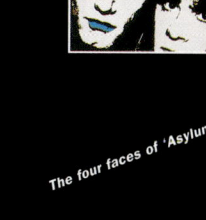

★ While Art was causing lively debate in the Big Apple, the second and final leg of Kiss' US 'Animalize' tour was coming to a spectacular finish at the sold-out Brendan Byrne Arena in East Rutherford, New Jersey on March 29. With the album that spawned the trek now a platinum seller, and the official release of the *Animalize – Live Uncensored* video due on April 19 to boost the coffers even more, Kiss could finally relax for a while, and plot their next move. And, maybe, if we were lucky, confirm who their next guitarist was going to be.

★ Actually, the answer to that question wasn't that long in coming. On July 14, a heavily modified 'Creatures Of The Night' was distributed to stores. Featuring re-mixes of the album's title track, the mournful 'I Still Love You' and the glorious 'War Machine', the LP also sported a brand new picture sleeve. And that sleeve rather neatly solved the riddle as to who had been chosen to replace poor old Mark St. John within the Kiss ranks. There, amongst Gene, Paul and Eric's familiar faces, sat a sullen looking youth, decked out in white leopard-skin pants and a designer dog-collar. His name, Bruce Kulick.

★ That Kiss had elected to take on Bruce came as no big surprise to anyone who had seen or heard him on the 'Animalize' tour. Though a graduate of the Eddie Van Halen school of slash and burn, Kulick also counted veteran guitar heroes such as Jimi Hendrix and Jimmy Page amongst his influences, and this winning combination of past and present fused well within Kiss' decade-spanning sound. Fiery, intense and technically accomplished, Bruce Kulick's sonic flights were just what the group needed to keep them ahead of the game in the musically competitive Eighties.

★ Kiss were not however, the first band to benefit from the guitarist's capabilities - Kulick actually cut his rock'n'roll teeth with a bunch of young hopefuls named Blackjack. Featuring future soul superstar Michael Bolton on vocals, the combo had recorded two albums – a self-titled debut and 'Worlds Apart', in 1979 and 1980, respectively – before Bolton, leaving to pursue a solo career, put them on ice. Bruce, taking a lead from his older brother Bob, would enter the lucrative world of session work to earn a crust (cutting LPs with the likes of AOR supremo Billy Squier and The Good Rats) before receiving the Kiss call in 1985.

★ A modest, self-deprecating character, when once asked what theme his face-paint would have taken should he have joined Kiss in their earlier incarnation, his answer was both humorous and pretension-free.

★ "If it was up to me, I'd probably just put dog make-up on, and be the dog of the band."

★ Modesty aside, Bruce Kulick's guitaristic charms had certainly impressed Kiss enough to offer him the job, and when the group faced the press they were brimming with praise for their latest addition.

★ "Bruce is really a charm." said an enthusiastic Paul Stanley, "We were really lucky, because he's a joy to work with. It's just worked out so well with him. I can never see him going anywhere. Hopefully, he'll be here as long as I will. Mark St. John was supposed to join us on the European tour and he just never got better. Now he's OK, but besides being a little late, Bruce has spent quite

a bit of time with us and the chemistry that's developed is not something we will sacrifice. It was fate, just the way it worked out."

★ A workable unit once again, Kiss wasted little time getting back into the studio. Taking over second home Electric LadyLand in New York, they recorded 10 songs in all between June and July. The result of their efforts –

'ASYLUM'

– was in the can and ready for release by September 16 1985.

The four faces of 'Asylum'

★ Co-produced by Paul Stanley and Gene Simmons (the former being the main man behind the console), *Asylum* wasn't a bad record, just a little...uneven. The anthemic opener 'King Of The Mountain' was convincing enough, as was the semi-tender raunch of 'Who Wants To Be Lonely', but other fare such as 'Radar For Love' (or 'Black Dog 2' as it should have been called) and the tuneless 'Any Way You Slice It' let the momentum down, sounding more like late night jams than finely crafted rock songs. That said, the fast-paced, roof-raising 'I'm Alive' and catchy, semi-balladic 'Tears Are Falling' did contain genuine power, and as a result, pulled the album out of ordinary status.

★ Also on the plus side was the strength of the instrumental performances present. Carr and Kulick made as fine a musical partnership as Simmons and Stanley. Dove-tailing in and out of tempos, casually tossing off solos and breaks with a dare-devil's grace, Kiss' latest tag team could turn the most mundane chord progression into an interesting aural diversion. Yet, as good as Eric and Bruce were together, not even they could save the appalling 'Uh! All Night' from itself. An abrasive ode to the joys of the libido, the tune's lyrical sexism and sheer dumbness were an insult to all concerned:

★ "When you work all day you've got to UH! all night," proclaimed a salivating Simmons, slowly reeling in his tongue.

★ Believe it or not, it took the combined talents of three men to come up with that chorus: Gene, song-doctor Desmond Child and band buddy Jean Beauvoir. Kiss had scraped the poetic barrel before, but 'Uh All Night' was a new low...

★ An LP of extremities, 'Asylum' reached a respectable No.20 in the US charts, and a favourable No.12 in the UK. Producing a semi-hit single with 'Tears Are Falling' (No.51 US/No.57 UK), it again did the trick of keeping Kiss afloat as a hard rock force while so many of their contemporaries fell by the wayside. You had to give it to Gene and Paul – they had staying power.

★ On November 29, the inevitable Stateside 'Asylum' tour opened in Little Rock, Arkansas. In keeping with the group's policy of 'bigger, better, brasher', the new show boasted the largest Kiss sign ever, a staggering 40' x 20'. Originally planning to use the primary colours present on 'Asylum's sleeve as a theme for the stage-set, Kiss soon dropped the idea in favour of state-of-the-art technology – thereby turning what would have been a red, blue and yellow debacle into a multi-coloured fiesta of blinding lights, deafening explosions and fire-breathing splendour. Wise choice.

★ Yet, as the tour progressed into December 1985, a darker cloud appeared on the horizon. In a straightforward business deal, Kiss were asked to follow in the footsteps of bands such as Queen and play at the pleasure haven Sun City in South Africa. Promised an astronomical figure for one concert, the only clause would be a segregated

audience. Blacks one side, whites the other. To their enduring credit, the group refused point blank to even entertain the concept, proving not only that money couldn't buy their favours, but that they fully understood the inhumanity of the apartheid regime. Pity Queen couldn't say the same thing.

★ On the road for five months this time, April 11, 1986 saw the 'Asylum' tour wrapped up for good at Meadowlands Arena, New Jersey. Not straying from America once, Kiss had still managed to turn a healthy profit from their endeavours. Playing old 'haunts' such as New York's Madison Square Garden and the L.A Forum, they were once again a major concert attraction in the USA, and this time without the make-up. The decision to unmask had worked. Nonetheless, there wasn't an opportunity for a ticker tape parade as yet, as the band were about to embark on one of the most eventful years in their life.

★ As spring broke, rumours were abound in the music press of changes within the Kiss camp. Solo projects, radical new directions, you name it, journalists were writing about it. The only quantifiable truth to be confirmed though, was the band's involvement with the *Hear 'N' Aid* album. A heavy metal equivalent to Bob Geldof's 'Band Aid' and 'Live Aid' projects, the LP was designed to raise funds and public awareness for the victims of the harrowing Ethiopian famine. Organised by one time Rainbow/Black Sabbath vocalist Ronnie James Dio, *Hear 'N' Aid* was to be a varied collection of tracks from the giants of rock. Eager to help, Kiss contributed a live version of their tune 'Heaven's On Fire' to the cause. Gladly accepted by Dio, the song made the album, which was released in May 1986 to reasonable success.

★ Meantime, some of those much written about rumours were starting to see light of day. The ever-diverse Gene Simmons was indeed going solo – but only on the production front. Working with Los Angeles sleaze rockers Black 'N Blue, Simmons had agreed to oversee recording duties for the band's debut album on Geffen Records. Unfortunately, Black 'N Blue's career was short-lived, the public reluctant to respond to their particular gifts. There was one silver lined cloud though: group guitarist Tommy Thayer got on so well with Gene, he eventually secured a job as a Kiss roadie. All's well that ends well. The Black 'N Blue sessions weren't the end for Simmons foray into production. The workaholic bassist would also lend a hand to recorded efforts from former Plasmatics vocalist Wendy O. Williams and US bump and grinders Keel. Does that man stop?

★ Evidently not, as he and the other members of Kiss got together during the summer to film their second long form video, *Exposed*. Stuffed with interviews, scantily clad ladies, plenty of vintage live footage and a hysterically funny 'Paul Stanley Workout' routine, where the Star-Child demonstrates various positions never to be found on the *Exercise with Cindy Crawford* tape, it's well worth a look. Continuing the frenetic round of activity, Bruce Kulick took time out to record an instructional video for the *Hot Licks* guitar tutorial series and, not to be outdone, Eric Carr laid plans for a similar guide for drummers. It seemed that to Kiss, a change was as good as a rest.

★ Towards the end of the year, amid reports that the band might soon be ready to get back to recording again, Eric Carr got his first real taste of the perils of trusting English journalists with anything. Inviting a press photographer to a 'private' photo shoot in his bathtub (you can guess), the skinsman was somewhat surprised to find his well-scrubbed face glaring out from amongst the bubbles one week later in the pages of a popular British weekly magazine. Suffice to say, Eric remained 'unavailable for comment'.

★ And so to 1987. Enjoying the longest lay-off of their career, and still unwilling to confirm the date of their return to duty, Paul Stanley kept the holiday flag flying when in February, he joined Poison on-stage in Texas for a rave-up version of 'Strutter'. A fast-rising LA glam rock band, clearly influenced by Kiss in both style and sound, Paul's appearance with the group prompted gossip that he might well be producing their second album. Stanley had expressed interest, and Poison were keen for the alliance to happen, but would there be time? You see, on March 1, vacation really was over. Kiss were due in One On One recording studios in Los Angeles with producer Ron Nevison to begin pre-production work on a new album - their first in nearly two years. Working title - 'Who Dares Wins'.

★ Calling in all hands, Gene Simmons was actually the last to make it back for the new project. Finishing up production duties of his own with Japanese act E-Z-O (a metallic foursome who coincidentally sported face paint not unlike Kiss), he barely had time to get out his photo collection before getting to the studio.

★ Yet, while Kiss remained hidden at One On One with Ron Nevison, their public profile continued to rise. Releasing the recently filmed *Exposed* to stores on May 18, the group were chuffed to hear they had a runaway hit on their hands. The raunchy combination of pool-side babes, classic Kiss footage and self-deprecating humour was obviously just what the doctor ordered as sales of the video soared to platinum status within a month. Another illustration of Kiss' ability to manipulate promotional tools to their advantage, *Exposed*'s success neatly prepared the rock market for the band's imminent comeback. Still, it wasn't enough for certain factions of the Kiss Army. The spectacular footage of the original line-up pacing the boards in the video prompted rumours of a reunion tour once again, with Ace and Peter returning to don the make-up and stack heels. It was clearly nonsense, as both Kiss Mark Five and Frehley were about to release new LPs, but you couldn't blame the fans for trying. After all, that grainy film clip of the first Kiss model performing 'Deuce' in San Francisco *circa* 1975 contained more energy and enthusiasm than the majority of their Eighties output thus far.

★ Taking a temporary break from recording the new LP, Paul Stanley flew out to the Dallas' Cottonbowl Stadium to join Poison on stage. Tearing through 'Strutter' part two before 80,000 mad Texans, the liaison refuelled gossip that Paul really was going to produce Poison's next record. However, like the fabricated story of Kiss' reunion tour, it was all hot air. Veteran producer Ron Werman was to take the job in the end.

★ Preparing for their real return, Kiss were interviewed at the Long Beach California radio station KNAC on August 5, where they invited fans to be part of the filming of a video for their new single, 'Crazy, Crazy Nights', to be shot in downtown Los Angeles the following Saturday afternoon. Three thousand fans eventually accepted the invitation, packing LA's Olympic Auditorium for the party. Rewarded with a special free concert afterwards, 300 of the throng also received one-of-a-kind T-shirts commemorating the occasion. That wasn't all. Two especially faithful Kiss acolytes were lucky enough to be presented with Gene Simmons' bass and Paul Stanley's guitar. Reports that the recipients of these much sought after prizes were blonde, busty and eager to show their gratitude were probably correct.

★ At last, on September 18, Kiss' latest LP was released.

Tying in with the soon to come single, it was called

'CRAZY NIGHTS' and hopes were high for a

million seller. An inconsistent album, its main highlights

were Paul's hard-hitting rocker 'Walls Come Down', the

gentle 'Reason To Live', 'Thief In the Night' (first recorded

by one-time Plasmatics vocalist Wendy O. Williams) and

the insistent, good time feel of 'Turn On The Night'.

Unfortunately on the down side, songs such as 'Hell To

Hold You', 'Bang Bang You', and 'My Way' seemed nothing

more than filler material, lead booted parodies of the former

★ The dichotomy was nowhere more apparent than in the polar opposites of 'Hell Or High Water' and the record's title track, 'Crazy, Crazy Nights'. Where the former – a growling slice of moody rock'n'roll, penned by Gene and Bruce – bristled with tension and mean spirits, propelling itself along on the back of a superb Simmons vocal and Paul's iron-lunged chorus fills, the latter, well... it just fizzled. 'Crazy, Crazy Nights' summed up, in one song, what was wrong with the Kiss of the Eighties. Yes, it was catchy, yes, it was anthemic, yes, it was probably going to be a hit. But it could have been anyone – from Bon Jovi to Great White, from Ratt to Quiet Riot. A faceless tune designed for the radio, 'Crazy, Crazy Nights' had all the character and drive of a soft-drinks commercial. And worse still, you couldn't stop singing the bloody thing.

★ Within the space of a decade Kiss had gone from leading the pack to driving alongside it. That they still had the old fighting spirit wasn't in doubt – the killer vibe of 'Hell Or High Water' was proof enough – but if the band were again to resemble wolves rather than poodles, they'd have to get back some of that hunger of the Seventies.

★ Perhaps the fault lay with the lack of co-writes between Gene and Paul. The pairing that had produced such classics as 'Strutter', 'Rock And Roll All Nite' and '100,000 Years' had long ago elected to work with other songsmiths rather than each other. According to Stanley, the division would not be repaired. "We don't write together because we see things differently. And one of the freedoms that we have at this point is being able to see a song through totally the way we want it to be," said Paul. "If we worked together I'd feel a little cheated, because Gene's approach is different and vice versa. I think that makes for a more varied feel to the record, a wider perspective, because we're not just metal, we're not just rock, we are ourselves and our limitations are only what we impose on ourselves."

★ While his remarks made sense, why did they still feel the need to replace each other with outside contributors? After all, some of Kiss best tunes were actually written solo. Gene had a fine track record of self-penned songs – 'Deuce', 'Calling Dr. Love' and *Hotter Than Hell*'s thrilling 'All The Way' were all his own work – and Paul similarly had added 'Got To Choose', 'Black Diamond' and the gorgeous 'Firehouse' to the classics list. By introducing the likes of Desmond 'catchy chorus' Child and Adam 'where's the melody' Mitchell to the creative pot, they were distilling great individual ideas in favour of a democratic hotch-potch.

★ Gene Simmons would later admit that much of Kiss' output in the Eighties was disappointing. Blaming both himself and the climate of the times, his admissions were candid and painful to hear: "I considered myself to be a joke in the Eighties and the music in general that we made was a load of crap. It was a dangerous time, when music was dictated to by record companies, and the people who ran them had never been to a concert – backstage doesn't count – let alone been in a band. Our own records in the Eighties were horrendous, but oddly they continued to sell. We were blessed, but we had no right to be."

★ *Crazy Nights* took Kiss to No.18 in the US charts, and No.14 in the UK. The single 'Crazy, Crazy Nights' also brought success. Acting as an anodyne advertisement for the

album – it hit No.65 in the States and an astonishing No.4 in Great Britain (Kiss' highest ever chart placing there) – the tune ensured that by the end of 1987, the group's overall sales had topped a staggering 70 million copies.

★ Amid all the palaver, Gene Simmons announced that he planned to launch his own record label, Radioactive Records, to be distributed through PolyGram, but Ace Frehley wasn't on the roster. Releasing his long-awaited debut album – *Frehley's Comet* – some months before on Megaforce Records, Ace was far too busy playing the New York circuit in support of his own effort to take any notice of Gene's plans. An impressive, if slight disc, *Frehley's Comet* was strong on attitude, if a little lacking in musical fibre. Tracks like 'Breakout', 'We Got Your Rock' and the instrumental reprise of his own haunting 'Fractured Mirror' – 'Fractured Too' – were all class stuff, but other fare such as 'Dolls' and the uninteresting 'Calling To You' did let down the side a little. That said, Ace's abusive guitar sound had been captured well by producer Eddie Kramer, and in the autobiographical 'Rock Soldiers', Frehley had written a bona-fide classic. With an enviable gift for lyrical word-play, the Ace from Space had managed to turn his near death experience behind the wheel of a DeLorean on the Bronx's River Parkway into a laconic and humorous statement of intent: "When I think of how my life was spared from that near-fatal wreck, if the Devil wants to play his card game now, he's gonna play without an Ace in his deck..."

★ On November 14, the *Crazy Nights* world tour opened in Pensacola, Florida, at the Bayfront Auditorium. Supporting Kiss on the trek were Queens-born Anthrax, a charmingly named act who were just starting to make major waves with their savage combination of thrash metal speed and semi-rapped vocals. As usual, Kiss had elected to take out a group who could potentially give them a real

run for their money. But as Anthrax grew to learn, nobody could touch the veterans on the live stage. Strong rumours were circulating that Kiss might use this jaunt to record an *Alive III* concert set, but fans would actually have to wait some six more years for that privilege. Not to be silenced, though, the Kiss Army still asked questions about a new live

tour is on other people's minds, but not ours."

★ As the irritating sound of 'Crazy, Crazy Nights' reverberated around arenas world-wide, Gene Simmons must have had a hard time concentrating. After all, when this latest on-the-road party was over, he had the difficult task of setting up his new label. Now called $immons Records, instead of Radioactive, the work that had to go into the enterprise was bound to be a thankless task until the profits started rolling in. However, Gene's ambitions, hard to realise or not, at least made sense. Musician, actor and now company executive, Simmons had in fact discovered no less than three bands that in the long term would achieve varying degrees of success: Angel, signed to Casablance in the mid-Seventies; Mammoth, who eventually changed their name to Van Halen; and Cinderella, who released a string of platinum albums throughout the mid-to-late Eighties.

★ With this track record, it seemed that Gene's foray into artist development was guaranteed to be a money spinner. Yet, the label was over almost before it began. Like those acting aspirations of his, Simmons found that to really do the project justice, he'd have to devote all his time and energies to it. Unwilling to abandon the love of his life, namely Kiss, the bassist reluctantly dropped his plans and concentrated instead on the business of writing songs for the group.

★ Thankfully, Gene could console himself with the next item on the Kiss agenda – Castle Donington. In August 1988, the group returned to the UK to play the Monsters Of Rock Festival before a capacity crowd of 98,700 fans. Second on the bill to Romford rockers Iron Maiden, former Van Halen frontman David Lee Roth, Megadeth and Helloween were all also appearing. However, despite sterling performances from many of the acts, the event was forever to be marred by tragedy. On the wettest day in the history of the festival, two fans died during up-and-coming LA group Guns N' Roses' set, because of the crowd crushing forward on a very slippery surface. What Simmons and Co. had hoped would be a celebration in the sun had turned into a terrible calamity most wished to forget.

★ Kiss' visit to England wasn't all bad, though. They achieved another career landmark when, in early September, they became the first band to play at London's famous Marquee Club, opening new premises in Charing Cross Road. Upgraded from its previous 400-capacity location in Wardour Street (where it had established a reputation as one of the world's most influential rock venues), the club could hardly have had a more auspicious

tour of the US, due to start in February 1989. Performing a pot pourri of his own Kiss songs, coupled with selected cover versions such as Led Zep's 'Communication Breakdown', the dates would realise a long held ambition of the Star Child's to hit the stage under his own steam. Destined to become a tremendous critical and commercial success, Paul's solo outing brought to the attention of many just how charismatic a frontman he really was. Combining enviable stage presence with a passion for performance, Stanley's persona would engulf the small venues he played. Sadly, the tour was just for kicks, and a live album of the concerts (bootlegs aside) was never considered.

★ Meanwhile, as Paul got ready for his moment in the solo spotlight, Kiss decided to end the year with the release of yet another compilation LP. Entitled

'SMASHES, THRASHES & HITS' it hit

the stores in December and reached a respectable No.21 in the US, but stiffed in the UK at a disappointing No.62. Featuring 13 newly re-mixed/mastered versions of old Kiss classics, including Eric Carr's vocal take of Peter Criss' weepy ballad 'Beth', the album actually wasn't that bad, and with two freshly recorded Paul Stanley tunes – the virginal 'Let's Put The 'X' In Sex' and priestly '(You Make Me) Rock Hard' – added to sweeten sales, it should have done considerably better in Kiss' domestic market. Still, just how many times can you buy 'Love Gun' ?

★ The complication was the last product issued under the band's original contract with Mercury/PolyGram. Kiss would re-sign a financially more lucrative deal with the same label within months of the release of Smashes... And so to Christmas once again. Kiss as an entity had now been around 15 years in all. A law unto themselves in most ways, inventing new rules as they progressed, what could possibly put a dent in that formidable armour? Unfortunately, it was only a matter of time before we all found out.

Facing Page:
The inimitable Paul Stanley

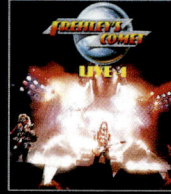

had been a busy boy in the last two years. Releasing an EP, *Live Plus One*, plus two more albums, *Second Sighting* and *Trouble Walkin'*, the guitarist's prolific output was quite at odds with the laid-back image he had cultivated. While former Kiss mucker Peter Criss had all but disappeared from the music scene, Ace had kept the space flag flying in style. However, sales of his LPs were hardly setting records. Though his material was worthy, retaining much of the flair and humour of his glory days, it seemed that Frehley's appeal lay solely with the faithful few who had followed his star since leaving Kiss in 1982. With no hit single to reactivate interest in his activities, and his original audience now having to deal with nappies rather than smoking Les Pauls, any hopes of world domination were receding fast. Still, he could easily live off the royalties generated by the Kiss back catalogue, and burning down smaller venues when the mood took him.

★ Which is precisely what the Spaceman was doing on May 4, 1989, at the Palace in Hollywood, California. Finishing the concert trail that had started a month or so before, Ace was playing to a packed and appreciative house, with some celebrities on hand too; two rather famous ones in fact, namely Gene Simmons and Bruce Kulick. But if the fans were expecting the threesome to tear through a hard-hitting 'Deuce' or more appropriately a drunken 'Cold Gin', they would wait in vain. Content to watch his former colleague from the safety of the bar, Simmons and new axe-slinger Kulick stayed well away from the stage, admiring rather than participating. That reunion would have to wait.

★ Vacation and astronomical observations over, Kiss regrouped at Fortress Recording Studios in LA to begin work on the follow-up to *Crazy Nights*. Happy with the new deal cut with Mercury/PolyGram – a 10-year commitment, seven albums to be delivered, including solo projects from Simmons and Stanley (which never materialised), plus more greatest hits packages and an *Alive III* for good measure – things were looking good for the combo. With a plethora of fresh material written in the lay off, and Stanley hot off the road and in fine vocal form, this album might even hit double platinum.

★ Never ones to take longer than absolutely necessary

in the studios, Kiss were soon out shooting a video for

their first single from the new album, 'Hide Your Heart'.

Filmed atop the Wiltshire Hotel in downtown Los Angeles,

the promo was a real angst-ridden affair, following Paul's

lyric of forbidden passion between two star-crossed lovers.

stations in October to warm up the market for the album.

Entitled 'HOT IN THE SHADE' it was due in

the stores in November. That same month, they were

back on TV as guest hosts of MTV's *Headbangers' Ball*.

Unsurprisingly, *Hot In The Shade* was hot on the agenda.

★ As good as their word, the new disc hit the racks before November was out. Unfortunately, despite all the pre-release hype, it provided Kiss with their poorest chart placing for a new studio effort in years, reaching only No.35 in the States and No.29 in the UK. The band must have been mighty peeved by the reception, and somewhat confused too, because the album wasn't really that bad. The joyous opening track 'Rise To It' might have lacked lyrical inspiration, but more than made up for that in punch. Growing from a bluesy slide guitar intro into a sprawling hard rock workout, 'Rise To It' was a corking way to set things in motion. It was followed by Gene's high-octane 'Betrayed' and single in waiting 'Hide Your Heart'. The momentum and energy level generated by these three tracks was higher than anything the band had put out since *Creatures Of The Night* in 1982.

★ Unfortunately, that velocity couldn't be sustained, and the following trio of 'Prisoner Of Love', 'Read My Body' and 'Love's A Slap In The Face' all crash-landed rather badly. Things picked up again with the tender power ballad 'Forever' and the snarling 'Silver Spoon', but it wasn't long before the likes of 'Cadillac Dreams', 'The Street Giveth And The Street Taketh Away' and 'Somewhere Between Heaven And Hell' again dropped the pace. Eventually ending on the clever instrumental histrionics of Gene and Bruce's 'Boomerang', *Hot In The Shade* was a work of two distinct tones – one bright and breezy, the other tired and limp. Not bad, but not that great either.

★ Still, with 'Forever', Kiss did have a gold-plated hit waiting patiently in the wings. While 'Hide Your Heart' and 'Rise To It' would make only modest impressions on the singles chart, the evocative nature of the Stanley/Michael Bolton written ballad ensured Kiss had a place in the sun after all. Settling at No.8 in the US Top 10, (it inexplicably stalled at No.65 in the UK), 'Forever' allowed Kiss the luxury of their highest singles chart placing in 14 years, and a more positive public profile than their latest effort probably deserved.

★ There were valid reasons why both 'Hide Your Heart' and 'Rise To It' failed to sky-rocket into the upper echelons of the Hot 100. In the former's case, there were no less than four versions of the tune doing the rounds – one by British chanteuse Bonnie Tyler, the other three by Southern Fried Molly Hatchet, Coca-Cola commercial girl Robin Beck and Kiss, of course – and when a song has to compete against itself at that level, it seldom has a hope. With 'Rise To It',

COOL LEON AND THE CRACKED RIBS

the logic is a little different, but just as compelling. A lively stomper, backed by a video where Gene and Paul had actually put the make-up back on for a few moments, you'd have thought the song stood a great chance. But following a huge hit like 'Forever' can be difficult, and the stompability factor of 'Rise To It' simply didn't lull the customers into the same sweet submission that its gentle predecessor had. Maybe it was just the fact that casual fans didn't find the tunes interesting enough, but these were two of the better singles Kiss had produced in a largely barren decade.

★ While *Hot In The Shade*'s singles awaited their shot at chart action, a far stranger drama was being waged in the pages of the *Star*. Leading with the headline 'Kiss Drummer Hits The Skids' the newspaper claimed in December 1988 that Peter Criss was now a homeless alcoholic, dependent on the charity of others to make it through the day. In the event, the story was complete fabrication. The drunken percussionist turned out to be an impostor named Christopher Dickinson, who had posed as Criss for a quick buck. Understandably irked by the negative publicity, the real Peter emerged from the shadows to file suit against the paper, which was settled out of court for an undisclosed sum.

★ In the same month that Peter found himself back in the headlines, Kiss released a promotional EP called `FIRST KISS LAST LICKS` to radio stations. A vinyl only compilation, featuring original demo versions of 'Deuce' and 'Strutter' from June 1973, and a remix of the previously unavailable 'Nowhere To Run', there were only 800 copies pressed of the EP in all – making it one of the rarest pieces of Kiss memorabilia available. Designed to commemorate the band's 15th anniversary, and draw attention to the forthcoming tour, 'Last Licks' is now worth a lot of money.

★ In preparation for their imminent excursion into US arenas, Kiss played a benefit show at the Stone Pony club in Asbury Park, New Jersey on April 14. Pleased with the response they received, Kiss went one better on April 24, playing a free show for 200 contest winners from all over California at the Country Club in Reseda. Performing 26 songs in all – the longest set in their history – they were, by the end of the night, more than ready for an eight-month haul across North America. Incidentally, the Reseda show premièred the first (and last) live performance of Eric Carr's tune 'Little Caesar'.

★ And so to the road. On May 4, the tour opened at the Coliseum, Lubbock, Texas. The stage set built to accompany the group was their largest yet, featuring a 40-foot high by

70-foot wide sphinx, from whose mouth Kiss emerged at the start of the show. Leon (the name given to the monument) also shot lasers from his eyes and even got to sing part of 'God Of Thunder'. The mind boggles. Yet however marvellous Kiss' ninth wonder of the world was, it couldn't protect Paul Stanley from himself. Running at full speed into a piece of jutting metal during one of his more athletic forays, the agile singer managed to crack several of his ribs, forcing Kiss to cancel a handful of dates. That wasn't the end of the Star-Child's bad luck: while *en route* to New York on July 4, Paul was involved in a massive road accident. Although his car was a complete write-off, Stanley somehow made it out alive, sustaining only minor injuries. That said, more shows were cancelled while he recuperated at home.

★ Mishaps aside, Kiss finally got through the gruelling tour more or less in one piece, even managing to finish the job in some style at New York's Madison Square Garden on November 9. Promising those in attendance that they would return two years later to celebrate their 20th anniversary there, little did they realise at the time that this was to be Eric Carr's last show with Kiss. Tragedy was about to strike.

★ Kiss were oblivious to it as yet though. In fact, Gene Simmons' only real worry as the group entered 1991 was strenuously denying rumours of an imminent reunion of the original line-up. Growing tired of being asked endlessly when Ace and Peter were coming home, his tone was curt in the extreme: "Every band has its golden era, but not everyone can keep up the marathon pace. Is my destiny limited to the shorter vision of my partners? Ace and Peter could have had solo careers and remained in the band. But they have to sleep in the beds they made for themselves. We miss them, but they fucked up big time – and they know it."

★ He would eat the words with lashings of salt within the space of five short years. Unfortunately, munching on hasty sentences would soon be the least significant of Kiss' problems...

10

In February 1991, Kiss went back to work. Demoing material for their new album, the band were hoping to capture as many ideas as possible before joining Bob 'Destroyer' Ezrin in the studio towards the end of the year. Having produced their last few efforts themselves, Gene and Paul now felt the time was right to bring in a fresh pair of ears, and Ezrin, responsible for one of the major successes of their career, was the man elected to steer the Kiss ship into chartable waters once again. Unfortunately, Eric Carr's involvement in the sessions was to be slight. Indeed, their drummer was fighting for his life.

★ Diagnosed as having a cancerous tumour on his heart, Eric underwent surgery to remove the growth on April 9. Unusual in a man so young (he was 40 at the time of the operation), all he could do was wait and see what the future would bring.

★ Keeping busy was probably the best medicine Kiss could find. Therefore the band found themselves cutting an old Argent song, 'God Gave Rock And Roll To You II', to contribute to the soundtrack of the forthcoming movie *Bill & Ted's Bogus Journey*. Having been thrown off a tour with the pomp-rockers in 1974 for being too wild, the tune might have seemed an odd choice for Kiss to make. But the wound was long forgotten, and besides, it was quite catchy. Produced by Bob Ezrin and featuring Eric Carr on backing vocals – he was too ill to play drums – the end result was a crisp, anthemic piece of power pop, with hit written all over it. Kiss' instincts regarding the track were proved right. On its release as a single in the UK, it reached a cracking No. 4.

★ But any joy to be had from 'God...' was brief. In August 1991, an official announcement came from the Kiss camp stating that Eric Carr was battling with cancer. Though the band and its associates had carried the knowledge of Eric's condition for some time, the news nevertheless came as a profound and distressing shock to fans and industry alike. By September, Carr's condition had declined so much that he had suffered the first of two brain aneurysms. His system weakened and his body was plagued by further complications from earlier surgery to remove the tumour. Eric Carr eventually died on November 24. He was 41.

★ The remaining members of Kiss were plunged into a state of shock. Not only had they lost one of the most accomplished and innovative drummers in rock, but more importantly, a close friend. He had shared in the successes of the last decade, brought humour and honesty when it was needed most and, above all, a loyalty and love of the music few could match.

★ "I was actually taking a week off in Hawaii, and I got the call in the middle of the night," recalled Paul soon after Eric's death. "I think everybody can understand without going into detail that it was a tremendous shock, and an incredible loss, and going into it further is not something I really want to share. It kind of cheapens something that's mine."

★ Gene, equally as shaken, gave a clearer indication of what the tragedy had meant to him and the group: "Eric never had an enemy in his life as far as I know. This was just a good guy. Anybody's death is tragic, but especially so in

Eric's case. It was a big blow to us, and not just emotionally. Musically, he was the engine of the band... but I'll tell you what, Eric's illness really made us take a second look at everything, not just our private lives, but also what this band is about."

★ Typically, Simmons chose to recall his friend by one of his greatest character traits – humour: "Eric would always pull pranks, especially on me for some reason. I guess because people tend to think I brood or sulk or whatever – this big dark guy. And Eric, every morning when we'd be at the airport, catching the next flight, he'd buy me a little silly, stupid stuffed toy, like a little kid's stuffed toy. A little bear, a little rabbit. And I'd have to walk through the airport with this pink, fluffy little animal that I'd be holding. Of course, people would be giving me real strange looks, and that's what he'd get off on. He loved pranks. That was Eric..."

★ In December, Kiss began their fight back from the grief of losing Eric. Assembling at the studio to lay down tracks for their forthcoming album with Bob Ezrin, it must have been hard to summon any real enthusiasm for the road ahead. However, salvation of a sort would come with the arrival of new drummer Eric Singer. The sticks behind Paul's solo tour, Cleveland-born Singer was already a veteran of the rock wars long before he had met Stanley. Learning his trade with performers as diverse as Lita Ford, Gary Moore, Alice Cooper, Badlands and Black Sabbath, Eric had by his own admission a 'Have sticks, will travel' kind of attitude until Kiss came calling. Like Eric Carr, he was an accomplished and committed musician, a huge fan of the band (he had seen Kiss many times as a youth in his hometown) and to Bruce Kulick's great delight, was a huge fan of guitar solos.

The much missed Eric Carr
Right: Eric Singer (seated) joins the Kiss ranks in 1991

ALL GOOD THINGS...

★ Driven by the fresh approach of their latest recruit and the wish to do Eric Carr's memory proud, Kiss tore into the making of what was to become known as 'REVENGE' Completing work on the record by March 1992, they celebrated by commencing a month-long club tour of the USA. Kicking off at the Stone in San Francisco on April 23, Eric Singer's début with Kiss showed the band attacking old and new material with a power not seen for years.

Was the hunger back?

★ On May 14, we found out for sure, as *Revenge* arrived in the stores. Quite simply the best Kiss album since *Creatures Of The Night*, *Revenge* marked a return to form many had thought impossible. Exorcising the ghost of their uneven and largely bland Eighties output in one blast, the album was a corker. It opened with a rumble of white noise, but the aural mists soon cleared to reveal the devastating grind that was 'Unholy' whose disturbing and malevolent lyrics outlined clearly the new regime:"I was there through the ages, chained snakes to their cages, I have seen you eat your own, I'm the cycle of pain of a thousand year old reign..."

★ Backed by Singer's unrelenting drums, and a solo flight from Kulick that stripped wallpaper with its seering tone, it was Simmons that stole the show. Growling, cantankerous, and downright spooky in his vocal delivery, the Devil was back, make no mistake.
★ Other material on show was just as strong. Paul's 'I Just Wanna' and 'Take It Off' were both anthemic killers in the old tradition, hot-wired examples of how powerful Stanley's voice could be given the right backing. But if there

was to be a stand-out moment on *Revenge* to accompany the rumble of 'Unholy', 'Domino' had to be it. A sleazy, politically incorrect slab of hard rock dynamics written by Gene, it would win no prizes from the feminist camp with its lyrics – "When that bitch bends over, I forget my name" – but with that masterful and incisive use of rhythm and space, you could easily forgive Simmons his fantasies.
★ *Revenge* ended with a tribute to the late Eric Carr in the form of 'Carr Jam 1981'. An unfinished demo held over from the *(Music From) The Elder* sessions – originally titled 'Heaven' – it actually had been co-written by the drummer with Ace Frehley. However, the version of the track that appeared on the LP had Ace's contributions wiped from it, and was therefore solely credited to Eric. Pernickety perhaps, in consideration of Frehley's legacy in the Kiss legend, but the song's inclusion nonetheless remains a moving gesture from his former colleagues. The album was dedicated to Eric.
★ *Revenge* gave Kiss the hit they had been searching for. Catapulting into the American charts at No.6, the album's strong showing ensured the group their highest ever placing in the Top Ten. Suffice to say, it went platinum. Yet *Revenge* wasn't only responsible for rejuvenating Kiss' place in the rock market. It also seemed to have performed a miracle on Gene Simmons. In his own words, Gene had spent much of the Eighties looking like... "A drag queen... Phyllis Diller's cousin... something I'd fucked the night before." Content to prance around the stage in bouffant hair-dos, creamy silk shirts and designer leather trousers, the singer bore more than a passing resemblance to the low rent hookers you found hanging around New York's 42nd Street. No more. Glaring out from the publicity stills that accompanied the release of *Revenge*, Gene was now more debauched Samurai than tacky call girl. Sporting an unkempt goatee beard, pervy ankle-length leather coat and studded boots, Simmons' new look was a breath of filthy, rock'n'roll air.
★ Rolling out the tour carpet in early May, Kiss performed eight sold-out shows throughout the UK, before taking a quick break to plan the US onslaught, beginning on October 1 in Allentown, Pennsylvania. Unfortunately, the band were backed by their least impressive stage set in recent memory. Yes, it included a Statue Of Liberty which fell apart during 'War Machine' to reveal a grinning metal skull, and sure, there were some semi-impressive laser displays on show, but nothing like the spectacle on previous jaunts. Nevertheless, as the dates progressed the band would come up with a novel solution for the absence of theatrics.
★ As they made their way across the USA, someone had the bright idea of employing strippers to disrobe during new song 'Take It Off'. And sure enough, before you could say the words 'bright furry G-String', stage was covered in more nubile flesh than you could shake a... stick at. Bringing a regular entourage of exotic dancers with them from town to town, Kiss soon found that every time they pulled into a new port, there were dozens more girls queueing up at the backstage door. It seemed wherever the group showed their faces, the request posed to them was the same: "Please let me lose my kit before 20,000 screaming rednecks." Unsurprisingly, the group themselves vetted the hopefuls.

taped shows in Detroit, Cleveland and Indianapolis for the upcoming `ALIVE III` album. These gigs were also filmed for release on video. *Kiss Confidential* features the engaging talents of several dancers of an exotic nature.

★ Despite the nightly flesh-fest that was taking place on the concert trail, the *Revenge* tour ground to a halt on December 20, in Phoenix, Arizona, due to poor ticket sales. With America at the mercy of grunge-mania, spearheaded by the likes of the blistering Nirvana, protest kings Pearl Jam and the caustic Stone Temple Pilots, the live market for Kiss' brand of good-time rock'n'roll was all but dying out. Even traditional heavy metal, usually unaffected by the vagaries of musical fashion, was under attack. Bands who swore by the old values, such as Judas Priest, Black Sabbath and Scorpions, found themselves crushed by the onslaught of harder, hipper alternatives: Alice In Chains, Pantera, Danzig. These stark, innovative acts practised little in the way of lyrical sexism, they seldom referred to headless corpses or wicked elves and they most certainly did not wear spandex. With only hardy perennials Aerosmith and Metallica seemingly unaffected by the changes that were sweeping through the States, Kiss took the hint and cancelled the second leg of their tour double quick. A re-think was surely in order.

★ Taking the bull by the horns, the band turned to what they knew best: self promotion. On February 25 1993, Kiss took a huge chance by allowing themselves to be interviewed by the scathing and controversial media figure Howard Stern on his nationally syndicated TV show. Due to the long-time feud that existed between Gene and the former shock-jock, sparks were expected to fly. But in reality, the verbal turf-war many had anticipated turned out instead to be a highly amusing and somewhat revelatory exercise in 'pubic' relations. Disclosing before the cameras that he had slept with the busty Jessica Hahn – another guest on the programme – Simmons not only took Stern by surprise (no mean feat), but also sealed his enduring reputation as rock's horniest toad. Toasting the victory by performing an acoustic version of 'Detroit Rock City' to rapt applause, Kiss stole the show from under the prominent nose of their host.

★ Obviously chuffed by their boys' latest *coup d'état*, Mercury Records put their money where their mouth was, and released the virgin single from the forthcoming *Alive III* on May 8. A rousing version of the *Creatures...* classic 'I Love It Loud', featured an accompanying video which was premièred on MTV the same week. Two weeks later, on May 18, Kiss' first live album in 15 years joined it on the racks.

★ *Alive III* was a faithful 16-track document of the *Revenge* tour, in all its wounded glory. Featuring storming versions of old war horses such as 'Deuce', 'Detroit Rock City' and 'Rock And Roll All Nite', the album also contained more contemporary aspects of the Kiss songbook, including 'Heaven's On Fire', 'Domino' and 'Unholy'. The band didn't forget the hits either: 'Forever' and 'God Gave Rock And Roll To You II' both appeared, but the biggest shock on show had to be 'Lick It Up', the title track from Kiss' first make-up free album, released a decade earlier. Freed from the constraints of its studio origins, the song crackled with life, building to its spiralling climax with a power and majesty only hinted at before. As with the two other *Alives*, audience participation was still at a premium. Master of Ceremonies Paul Stanley cut across the tracks with anecdotes, howls and cod-raps, and the album's upfront mix (courtesy of Eddie Kramer) made sure that all the crowd screams, whistles and 'Fuck Yeah!'s were prominently in place.

Simmons, Stanley & Kulick taking their 'Revenge' in 1992

★ Nevertheless, *Alive III* was never going to be as good as those two monster releases of the Seventies. *Alive* and *Alive II* were of a time when Kiss walked the Earth like demi-gods, a warped and blood-stained American answer to The Beatles before them. To expect the same response two decades on, when so much had changed for the band, would have been insane. Yet, on its own merits, *Alive III* was a good, if not truly great record. It proved Bruce Kulick had become an integral part of the Kiss sound, Eric Singer to be a stunning replacement for the much missed Eric Carr, and above all, that Gene and Paul could still pulverise an arena with their one-two punch. If allowed to grow, then this line-up had the makings of a classic rock'n'roll band.

★ *Alive III* débuted at No.9 in the US, pretty much matching its predecessors' chart placing all those years before. But while the original *Alives* had stuck around in the Top 30 for months, Kiss newest concert album soon trailed

★ Meanwhile, 1993 had seen Peter Criss emerge with a new band in tow. Releasing a five song EP by the end of the year, and a full on album some months after that, Peter was experiencing a bit of a renaissance. New songs such as – surprise – 'The Cat' and 'Show Me' were pretty good, and with tracks like 'Bad Attitude' and 'Blue Moon Over Brooklyn' re-uniting him with buddy Ace Frehley on lead guitar, the drummer had shown the world at large he was not a spent force. Criss just needed the right break...

★ Aside from providing edgy axe licks for Peter Criss' musical endeavours, and basking in the glow of the endless name checks he was being given by younger guitarists influenced by his style – try Snake Sabo, Dimebag Darrell, Kim Thayil, Anthrax's Scott Ian and Alice In Chain's Jerry Cantrell just for starters – Ace Frehley was building a second career as an artist. Always one for dabbling with a paint brush, he had now moved on to computer graphics, getting his first real exhibition at an art gallery in New Jersey. Working with a software package called Infini/D, Frehley had produced 14 pieces of work in all for the showing.

★ He was nothing if not honest about the origins of his talent. "I used to draw all the tattoos on everybody's arms," said Ace, referring to his gang days, "and in high school I designed the yearbook, and was always on the art staff. I can paint, water colour – all that stuff. But what attracts me to computer graphics is that there are no limitations – except your imagination."

★ It wasn't all sweetness and light in Space though. When Kiss were inducted into Rock 'n' Roll's Walk of Fame in May – leaving their hand prints for all time on Hollywood's Sunset Boulevard – Gene, Paul and Co. neglected to invite their former colleague to the party. Taking the slight badly, Frehley let fly with a scathing stream of invective, prompted he said, not only by the Walk Of Fame experience, but Paul and Gene's recent attitude in general. In an interview with *Guitar World*'s Jeff Kitts, Ace said: "It doesn't surprise me that they don't want me there. But they're only hurting themselves. I have fans constantly telling me that they've lost all respect for Paul and Gene because of the way they've been treating me lately. It only makes me realise how much I made the right choice when I left the band ten years ago.

★ "Let's face it, when I left the group, Kiss got a musical vasectomy. I was the original and the best, and they'll never be able to replace me. I was in Canada a few weeks ago, and Gene called me a moron in one of the local magazines. What the hell is his problem?... Is Gene trying to pick a fight with me? Shit, I'll meet him in Madison Square Garden if that's what he wants - name the date !"

★ Ace would eventually get to place those large hands of his in the cement on Sunset Boulevard, but it seemed he'd never again offer one to Gene and Paul in friendship. A fist, maybe, but certainly no shake. Things would change...

★ In Kissworld, the band were still plugging the charms of their latest release, *Alive III*. Paul was more than happy to explain why he thought the album was justified: "We always said that if we ever did *Alive III*, it would be some kind of retrospective, an event. Not just a live album. It would have been nice to tie it in with something special other than just a live concert. We didn't want it to be like *Jaws III*."

★ Continuing on the promotional trail Kiss had set off upon, the band appeared on TV show *Arsenio Hall* on May 20. Performing 'Detroit Rock City' and 'Deuce' to an audience of millions, they again showed a total command of the goggle-box. Answering fan's questions on a nationally syndicated live radio show, *Rockline*, on June 7, the group sounded relaxed and at ease. Hinting at a tribute album in the pipeline, little did listeners know that Kiss had already recorded a version of their gentle ballad 'Hard Luck Woman' with country star Garth Brooks, and were due to produce Lenny Kravitz's take on 'Deuce' the same month at Clinton Recording Studios in New York City. Lining up a star-studded homage to themselves, the name of the forthcoming self-tribute album was either to be *Great Expectations* or *Kiss My Ass*, depending on how brave they felt. Eventually, they would opt for brave.

Paul Stanley lets rip on his self designed Ibanez 'Iceman' guitar

★ On July 20, in amongst all this activity, *Kiss-Konfidential*, the long-form video document of the band's 1992 *Revenge* road-trip, arrived in stores. Incorporating most of the tracks from *Alive III*, classic footage from 1976/77 (namely live performances of 'Let Me Go, Rock And Roll', '100,000 Years' and 'Nothin' To Lose') and some saucy on-stage/backstage tomfoolery with those famous strippers, the film was an entertaining and lively record of a criminally neglected tour.

★ Appeasing the rabid fans who'd been knocking on their door since word had first got out about it, Kiss released details of the expected list of names for that upcoming tribute. Among others, the celebrity list included The Lemonheads, Megadeth, Nine Inch Nails, Extreme, Toad The Wet Sprocket, Guns N' Roses, Alice In Chains, Bell Biv Devoe, Anthrax, Soul Asylum, Lenny Kravitz, Garth Brooks and Stevie Wonder. However, many of the artists would not appear on the final product due to legal pressures from their record companies.

★ Barely stopping for air, Kiss headlined the 1993 Foundations Forum in Burbank, California on September 11. The Foundations Forum had become *the* meeting for the hard rock world, and musicians mingled freely with industry types and media people at the annual convention. Treating

the honour of headlining the event very seriously indeed, the band went into copious rehearsals. Performing their first full concert of the year, Kiss needn't have worried, as the partisan crowd were rocking in the aisles from song number one. Pulling out all the stops, the group even found time to air the exquisite 'Goin' Blind', the first time the tune had ever been played live in their history.

★ Closing the year with an appearance at Pleasure Island in Disney World, Florida, on December 12 for an upcoming TV special called *Dick Clark's New Years Rockin' Eve '94*, Kiss worked their way through three songs: 'Detroit Rock City', 'Makin' Love' and 'Rock And Roll All Nite'. Unfortunately, when ABC broadcasted the show on December 31, only two tracks made it on to the air, and for reasons best known to themselves, the network chose to present the footage of the group as a mirror image – instantly transforming Gene, Paul and Bruce into left-handed axe-wielders. Strange, but true.

★ Then radio silence. Fewer appearances than Bigfoot. What was happening? Breaking for four months from the promotional rounds that had accompanied *Alive III*, Kiss were actually concentrating on piecing together their pet project, the tribute album. Mindful of the market generated by similar homages to Led Zeppelin, Bob Dylan and The Carpenters, Kiss as usual had taken the initiative, and organised one of their own. Willing participants weren't found wanting. As the list they'd released showed, acts as diverse as Bell Biv Devoe and the glorious Soul Asylum were tripping over themselves (and their record companies, in these two's case) to get a piece of the action. What the critics had hated, a whole generation had been entranced by.

★ Unfortunately for Dave Pirner *et al*, contractual obligations meant that that they weren't going to make the final cut. Guns N' Roses too, missed the ship. But when 'KISS MY ASS' did finally appear on June 21, there were enough star performers present to ensure the album climbed to a very respectable No. 19 on the US charts.

Here's a run down of the LP from Paul and Gene:

1. DEUCE – Lenny Kravitz/Stevie Wonder
Gene: "I thought it was shocking, when I first heard it! I heard Lenny starting off the opening riff, then when the track came in and I heard the B3 and the Sly And The Stone Family stuff on top of it, it was like a breath of fresh air. I'd never imagined, in my wildest dreams, that 'Deuce' could sound like that."

2. HARD LUCK WOMEN – Garth Brooks with Kiss
Paul: "Garth said 'I want you guys to play with me'. We had no intention of getting that much hands-on with the album, but we wound up flying to Nashville to record in one of the country studios. He said he wanted to do it the way he and all the millions of Kiss fans remember it, so we did it as close as possible, 17 years later, and I think it's a better version. I think he sang his arse off, and we're real proud of it."

3. SHE – Anthrax
Gene: "They asked that we get involved and produce them. We said we really didn't want to do that, but they were very adamant. So we produced the thing, but it's very clearly Anthrax, very clearly that point of view. Very impressive."

4. CHRISTINE SIXTEEN – Gin Blossoms
Paul: "They've got that classic, almost Sixties jangle to the guitars. I think they've stayed fairly true to the original, but in the same way, it still sounds very much like Gin Blossoms."

5. ROCK & ROLL ALL NITE – Toad The Wet Sprocket
Gene: "Originally they were thinking of doing 'World Without Heroes', but changed their minds, because stylistically and in terms of tempo, it's closer to what they do, and they decided on this. They went, 'It's okay if we do it our way?', and we said, 'Yeah, take it all the way!' Nothing is sacred."

6. CALLING DR. LOVE – Shandi's Addiction (member of Rage Against The Machine, Faith No More and Tool)
Paul: "There's something exciting about getting members of different bands together on something where they all share a common view, and it's probably more exciting to have the members from three bands in that case then any one of those bands in particular. I think the tracksounds great – it pushes the envelope. It's like Kiss in the twilight zone."

7. GOIN' BLIND – Dinosaur Jr

Gene: "One of the first things J. Mascis said to me was. 'Do you mind if I put a cello quartet in there?' For a person to hear that in a song like this is obviously a unique point of view. I couldn't imagine how it was going to be used. First thing I thought of was like ELO or something, but it sounds nothing like that."

8. STRUTTER – Extreme

Paul: "The singing is great, the guitar playing is funky – they put their stamp on it, and they also added 'Shout It Out Loud' at the end. What can you say? It sounds like an Extreme song."

9. PLASTER CASTER – The Lemonheads

Gene: "For Evan Dando, who usually sings songs about heartbreak or being misunderstood, to sing a song called 'Plaster Caster', about fans who take plaster casts of your family jewels, is obviously a slice of life. It's obviously him banging away and having fun with the song. It's The Lemonheads all the way."

10. DETROIT ROCK CITY – The Mighty Mighty Bosstones

Paul: "I think these guys are the American cousins of Madness! It's got that whole vibe written all over it and to hear something like this with really out there, crazy horns on it and a vocal that sounds like somebody that gargles sand..."

Gene: "Somebody who just gargled Lemmy!"

11. BLACK DIAMOND – Yoshiki with 74-piece orchestra

Paul: "It's grandiose and it's a great way to end the album. It's like when the credits roll at the end of a film, you have a big orchestra piece that comes up – and that, I guess, is 'Black Diamond'."

★ But aside from Gene and Paul's glowing references, what was 'Kiss My Ass' really like? Diverse, interesting and above all, very entertaining. Bands like Anthrax and Extreme had captured Kiss' original swagger well, but also put enough of their own spin on the tunes to make them new again. Similarly, acts such as The Gin Blossoms and The Lemonheads brought an understated Nineties sensibility to their contributions, 'Christine Sixteen' and 'Plaster Caster'. Lenny Kravitz, with his funky, spare take on 'Deuce' (Stevie Wonder assisting on harmonica fills) showed what could be done when you weren't afraid of straying from your primary source, and for The Mighty Mighty Bosstones and Shandi's Addiction's irreverence was simply funny. The winners in the Kiss homage stakes though, had to be Dinosaur Jr., Yoshiki and Toad The Wet Sprocket. In Dinosaur Jr.'s case, J. Mascis' compelling and mournful treatment of 'Goin' Blind' was simply a revelation: a cello quartet underpinned the main melody while his world-weary voice slurred through verse and chorus. The tune really headed skywards when Mascis' howling lead guitar tore free from its gentle constraints. Yoshiki too, brought honour to his version of 'Black Diamond'. Conducting a 74-piece orchestra, the master musician brought previously unheard melodies and nuances into play, letting pianos, violins and horns do the work of guitars and bass. And in Toad The Wet Sprocket's case, well, you had the lot. Removing 'Rock And Roll All Nite' from its party setting completely, the band handed in a sumptuous country 'n' western ballad. Bitter-sweet, plaintive and emotionally charged, what had once been a up-tempo teen anthem was now almost a hymn. Gorgeous stuff.

The disc also featured a vicious speed-metal take on 'Unholy' by German hard-core band Die incorporating within its grooves a terrifying mid-track segue into Kiss' disco flirtation 'I Was Made For Lovin' You'. Listening to the singer switch from a gruff, growling basso profundo to a shrill, whistling falsetto within seconds, you'd swear you'd just walked onto the set of *The X Files*.

★ Kiss were justly proud of the record, giving credit to the innovation the acts had shown. "My jaw would drop when the material came in," says Simmons. "In our wildest dreams we couldn't have come up with the arrangements."

★ Stanley was equally gobsmacked: "You hear the songs on the album and they're new again, and stand and fall as songs. Like 'Rock And Roll All Nite' by Toad The Wet Sprocket became truly their own version, from their perspective."

at its core, ('Rock And Roll All Nite') was a campfire song." Robin Wilson of The Gin Blossoms confessed that his rock star fantasies were conceived while lip-synching to Kiss records, while Mighty Mighty Bosstones front man Dicky Barret offered a simple and effective explanation as to what had driven the Detroit band's take on Paul's ode to their city: "Kids growing up in the Seventies and Eighties had to be influenced by them one way or another."

★ Simmons admitted that the initial idea for the tribute album was prompted by *Hard To Believe* – a 1990 C/Z Records Kiss homage featuring artists like Nirvana and Bullet LaVolta, but sadly, unlike that compilation, *Kiss My Ass* had to deal with their politics of big business. Many of the groups that had lined up to participate had had their chances of appearing scuppered by contractual hassles. The Stone Temple Pilots, Nine Inch Nails, Skid Row, Alice In Chains – all failed to get a place on the final product due to clauses in their record contracts that expressly forbade dalliances with other labels. Wrecking those childhood dreams of joining their heroes in Kiss heaven, the likes of Scott Weiland and Trent Reznor must have been heartbroken.

★ Ace Frehley, too, almost put the kibosh on the project. Objecting to a likeness of his famous space make-up appearing on the sleeve, it seemed the guitar player still harboured a grudge regarding Gene's 'moron' comments. As a result of his protest, and the possibility of legal action from Frehley should the band not accede to his wishes, the album's cover deliberately blurred the Starman's face-paint – the child representing his character on the jacket turned to one side. In consideration of Ace's strong action, Paul Stanley was strangely kind to his former colleague: "It's really sad... because I'm sure Ace wouldn't have wanted to be a part of this, and I'd bet he didn't even know this guy who claimed to be his lawyer had done (it)."

★ Gene summed up the whole enterprise like so: "*Kiss My Ass* is the graduation of the Kiss Army. It's about

all those card-carrying members who were made fun of in school. It's about a guy like Lenny Kravitz, who was constantly ridiculed for being a Kiss fan. Well, guess what? Those people now have to buy tickets to see Lenny play."

★ On July 13, those ridiculed Kiss fans were jolted out of bed when the band made a surprise appearance on Jay Leno's *Tonight Show*, backing Garth Brooks' on his version of 'Hard Luck Woman'. Replaying his faithful and poignant rendition of the old Stanley tune, Garth brought down the house. Paul was especially happy to see the reaction, as Brook's interpretation of his tune had been his favourite moment on *Kiss My Ass*. Not wanting to take sides in the 'Who's better, Jay Leno or David Letterman?' debate, Simmons and Stanley also joined The Gin Blossoms on the top-rated TV programme *Late Show With David Letterman* to perform 'Christine Sixteen' some weeks later.

★ Continuing to make sporadic appearances (they'd managed two gigs earlier in the year), Kiss turned up next on July 30 in Nashville, as part of Gibson guitars' 100th anniversary celebrations. Performing on a floating stage, the band proved their ability to swim by not wearing water wings while stalking the wobbling boards.

★ In late August, Kiss returned to South America after a decade long absence on a 'Monsters Of Rock' stadium tour of Argentina, Brazil, Chile and Mexico with Suicidal Tendencies, Slayer and Black Sabbath. With Kiss topping the bill, Black Sabbath now realized how far they had fallen. In 1974, the gothic Brummies had been on an equal footing with Kiss, but now Tony Iommi and Co. had to be content to play second fiddle to the New Yorkers.

A quiet moment at rehearsals

★ Kiss may have spent their career singing about cars and girls – well, mostly girls – but it failed to mask the fact that behind the innuendo and double entendres, there operated two of the keenest and most intelligent minds to ever grace the rock business. But how many times could they continue to escape? After all, they'd hit their Forties. Children and wives needed to be fed. If Gene and Paul were to survive and prosper into the millennium, they'd have to

★ Returning home, Kiss continued to assuage the more fanatical of their supporters by producing the book *Kisstory*. After repeated requests from their tribe for an accurate chronicle of the band's life and loves, Gene and Paul had come up with an 8lb, 440 page bible of Kiss fact. One and a quarter feet long by one foot wide, and bound in its own protective case, the weighty tome was packed with unpublished photos from the group's private collection, plus little known stories concerning all members, and a great tattoos section where Kiss fanatics displayed a bewildering number of skin designs dedicated to Paul, Ace *et al*. A pricey $160, it was nevertheless a must-have item for thousands of the group's devotees. Sadly, they received some complaints when the seams of the book's initial run fell apart, but the guys were quick to correct the problem, issuing second, sturdier editions to those who had encountered the glitch.

★ Taking a lead from the success of their Australian convention dates, June 17 saw the beginning of the US leg of the Kiss Konvention tour. However, the Los Angeles chapter of the Kiss Army got more than they bargained for when old fur-features himself, Peter Criss, strolled on stage to take the mike for an emotional rendering of 'Beth'. Both shocking and delighting the assembled hordes, Criss' return started a rumour frenzy within minutes. Were the original line-up reforming? Would there be make-up? Was Ace coming back? Oh, please God let Ace come back, etc, etc, etc. If Gene and Paul knew the answers though, they weren't telling...

★ That same month, at least some indication was given to the faithful. With no sign of Simmons and Stanley, Peter Criss and Ace Frehley reunited for what was dubbed

had to re-learn much of their back catalogue to appease. And therein lay the secret. The devoted weren't screaming for Eighties material such as 'King Of Hearts' and 'Love's A Deadly Weapon', but for older, more obscure classics like 'Got To Choose' and 'Comin' Home'. Even the tribute bands who supported Kiss on the tour ignored their Eighties output. Preferring to wallow in the golden years, acts Hotter Than Hell and Cold Gin went down a storm because they were wearing make-up, spitting blood and firing rockets. Gene and Paul would have had to have been stupid not to see the demand for a reunion with Ace and Peter – and as we've found out, stupid was one thing they were not.

★ On August 9, 1995, the inevitable happened.

★ Performing for MTV's *Unplugged* show, Kiss Mark Six ran through a classy acoustic set, featuring such historical gems as 'Sure Know Something', 'Plaster Caster' and 'Got To Choose'. With the exception of *Revenge*'s corking 'Domino', the emphasis of the show was placed firmly in the past, and it was a delight to hear the likes of 'See You Tonite' and 'Do You Love Me' dusted down, and given a quick spin. Yet the band had saved the best for last. From out of the wings, for the first time in 15 years, appeared Ace Frehley and Peter Criss. The roar, needless to say, was deafening. Performing the tunes 'Beth' and '2000 Man' with Simmons and Stanley, the crowd's ecstatic response drummed home in no uncertain terms that *this* was the Kiss people wanted to see. As Bruce and Eric joined the reunited foursome for a roof-raising finale of 'Nothin' To Lose' and 'Rock And Roll All Nite', they must have felt like spare parts at a Hoover convention.

★ What had seemed an impromptu and reflex performance had in fact been orchestrated as carefully as a military operation. Assembling days before the broadcast at a New York rehearsal room, the sextet had thoroughly run through

11

REVENGE IS SWEET

the numbers until they were as tight as tuppence. But while Kulick, Stanley and Simmons experienced few problems with the stripped-down nature of *Unplugged* – they had, after all, been using non-electric instrumentation on the 'Kiss-Konvention' tour – Ace Frehley was kicking walls. Wanting to play his theme tune 'Shock Me' on the show, when Ace discovered that it was damn near impossible to bend strings on a jumbo acoustic guitar, let alone get it to feed back and fire rockets, he quickly compromised his choice to *Dynasty*'s '2000 Man'.

★ But was this meeting of giants a one-off? Well, it would have seemed that way when in November, Kiss – the Kulick/Singer model that is – headed back to the studios to start work on the follow up to the platinum selling *Revenge*. And with new albums also anticipated from Ace Frehley and Peter Criss (who were still on tour together) the signs for future collaborations were far from rosy. Simmons, for one, was having none of it: "There'd be no point to a reunion. I have nothing to prove in terms of performing, because the band is better live than it ever was. The truth is that today's Kiss buries the old Kiss. People may like the make-up and the look of old, but this is a much improved group that's playing better, singing better and which is lighter on its feet. But I guess if I was in Ace and Peter's position I would be claiming that a reunion's going to happen. It's a lot easier to say that than, 'Boy, did I fuck up'."

★ Keeping all in suspense, March 12 brought the release of the '**KISS UNPLUGGED**' album and home

video special. Produced by Alex Colleta, the CD sent shivers

down the spine: There for all to hear was the proof that

beneath the bluster, war-paint and spectacle, Kiss were

among the most talented songsmiths in the business.

Losing nothing from their acoustic setting, tunes such as

'Sure Know Something', 'Goin' Blind' and the tender

'Every Time I Look At You' simply shone, and with

'Rock And Roll All Nite' still as fresh as a daisy 20 years

after it was written, Kiss could rightly give the finger to any

critic that had accused them of being 'of their time'.

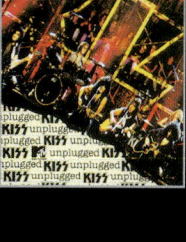

GENE SIMMONS PETER CRISS ACE FREHLEY PAUL STAN[

Together again after fifteen years, Kiss field questions from a ravenous press in 1996

★ But within five months of the *Unplugged* show, word started to leak out that the 'No way, no how' reunion tour might indeed be on. And by early February 1996, even those close to Kiss had given up trying to deny the rumours. Valentine's Day brought the answer in glorious technicolour. Completely side-stepping the press, an unbilled Ace, Gene, Paul and Peter turned up at the 1996 Grammy Awards in full make-up, wearing splendid variations on their 1977 *Love Gun* outfits. Presenting MOR act Hootie And The Blowfish with one of the awards up for grabs, when asked if they were back together, the only comment the group would offer was... "No comment."

★ Finally, on April 16, the waiting was over. Ending months of intrigue, speculation and gossip, Kiss announced their long-awaited reunion tour. Set to open on June 28 at Tiger Stadium in Detroit, with all four original members in place, you could hear the fans' whoops as far away as the middle of the Atlantic. That opening date in Detroit – 38,000 seats in all – sold out in an amazing 47 minutes, not only setting a new record for the venue, but inducing orgasms in promoters the length and breadth of the United States. Kiss were back.

★ Choosing low-key venue the USS Defiant to make the announcement, the group had brought with their return a sense of theatre that hasn't been present in rock 'n' roll in years. Promising to take the classic *Love Gun* stage set out of mothballs and bring it to a field near you, their flamboyance

the plaid shirts and sour faces of the professional moaners grunge had inspired. Yes, they were loud, yes, they did look faintly ridiculous, but these four men knew more about throwing a party than anyone. Confirming that they would headline the 1996 Donington Festival on August 17, and undertake a full European jaunt soon afterwards, the band also ended rumours that the comeback tour would only be a North American phenomenon. No, everybody was invited.

★ At first, it appeared that The Stone Temple Pilots would be the opening act for Kiss on the US tour, but after singer Scott Weiland was busted and ordered into a drug rehab centre during May 1996 for a minimum period of four months, STP couldn't commit. Alice In Chains would take up the challenge instead.

★ And so the race was on. Releasing a live compilation album entitled `YOU WANTED THE BEST, YOU GOT THE BEST!´ (sourced from *Alive!*, *Alive II* and some previously unreleased Seventies concert gems such as 'Two Timer' and 'Room Service') to coincide with their re-birth, Kiss finally hit the road, as promised, on June 28 at Detroit's Tiger Stadium. With front row tickets exchanging hands at a mind-blowing $7,000 a throw, expectations were great.

★ In a blaze of light, fire and explosions, Kiss took the roof off Detroit. Picking up exactly where they left off in 1977, the band looked and sounded like they had never been away. Dispensing with anything after their original glory year, Kiss crushed their audience with classic after classic: 'Deuce', 'Cold Gin', 'Makin' Love',

'Detroit Rock City', 'Let Me Go, Rock And Roll', 'Shock Me', 'Beth', 'Love Gun', 'Watchin' You', 'Rock And Roll All Nite', the list was endless. Fire was breathed, blood was spat, rockets were launched, drum-risers levitated and in a new gimmick, Gene Simmons shot from the stage on invisible wires into the lighting rig 30 feet above him to sing 'God Of Thunder'. The last time we'd seen anything like this, it was in the gatefold sleeve of *Alive II*. As the confetti reigned down around its head at the end of the set, Detroit knew the circus had come back to town.

★ It wasn't an isolated event. Nor a mirage. At Cleveland's Gund Arena, Kiss pulled it off again. And in Texas. Selling out 80,000 tickets in 58 minutes for their four-day homecoming at Madison Square Garden in July, they made grown men weep. The long neglected Generation W – that's the one before X – had once more found their messiahs, and were crawling out of the woodwork in millions to worship at their feet.

★ So what was involved in the resurrection? On the technical side, 13 convoy trucks, 500 pounds of confetti each night, 500 pounds of mild explosives – again, each night, daily operating costs of $250,000, and a road crew the size of Belgium. The band were even employing personal trainers to keep them in shape. But with earnings of approximately $900,000 per week from merchandising, and a potential gross of $50 million dollars from the tour, Kiss could breathe easy.

★ Was it the bucks that brought them back? That's a negative, according to Gene Simmons: "This reunion is not about money. It was the last thing on our minds. It really is *not, not* about money. Our rent's paid. We're doing it now because we don't have to worry about the money. All this is cream. Our biggest concern was not ticket sales or tour grosses. It was the fact that we have something very important to live up to. We have the faith and loyalty of fans who've been there over two decades. We can't just go through the motions. We have to give them something with jaw-dropping quality."

★ Still, at $85 a ticket, you had to wonder...

★ And so to Donington. Headlining the annual festival with Ozzy Osbourne, Sepultura, Biohazard, Dog Eat Dog, Paradise Lost and Fear Factory in tow, Kiss brought the whole kit and caboodle to England. Starting the show with a helicopter hovering 10 feet above the stage, they soon had the assembled thousands eating out of their hands with the fire-pots, smoke bombs, light show and that massive $40,000 bulb-eating logo pulsating above their heads. It wasn't just the audience that was impressed. Some of Kiss' fellow performers were in awe as well. Take Dog Eat Dog's Dave Neabore for instance: "I just shook hands with Gene Simmons and Paul Stanley. My life just came full circle."

★ Why was it that so many people felt this way about what effectively was four middle-aged guys in make-up? Paul tried to offer some explanation: "There's no doubt that your first recollection of something is your strongest. Put it this way: no matter how many James Bonds come along, most of us are gonna remember Sean Connery in the role, because he was the first. He defined the part. Ace and Peter, with Gene and I, with all of our positive and negatives, made Kiss what it was. The chemistry was unique to that line-up. There would be nothing more pleasing than if the four of us were here today, looking back at the last 20 years. But on the other side of the coin is that if the four of us had tried to stay together back then, the band wouldn't be here today."

★ Expanding his comments to explain the genesis of the reunion, the Star Child shed some real light on what had brought the quartet back together after all those years apart: "We got a chance to showcase the backbone of Kiss on the MTV *Unplugged* show, which is great songs. Songs will live or die by how they are perceived in their most stripped-down form. With acoustic guitars, you can't hide behind glitz and volume. If a song isn't good played on a single guitar, it's a crappy song. Doing *Unplugged* was a vindication. And it was phenomenal when we got together for the first time to rehearse. There was a certain amount of trepidation at first, but you're looking at four guys who at this point enjoy playing together.

★ "I think the world-wide Kiss conventions also played their role in getting us back together again. The cool thing about the convention is that it gave us a chance to celebrate our history and what we've accomplished. In looking at our past, we realised what a phenomenon Kiss has been for 20 years. That got us excited. And then doing *Unplugged* was like a family reunion. The true test of family is being able to overcome obstacles and find your way back. You look at each other and say there's too much good that happened and we shouldn't negate it by constantly being at each other's throats."

★ But what about the prodigal sons, Ace and Peter? Did they view it the same way? Frehley, as usual, was nothing if not straight-talking: "Once we did *Unplugged*, which was the first time the four of us had played together in 16 years, I think we all sensed that the chemistry was still there. At that point, we all knew there was a chance that this could work."

★ Peter, too, dwelt on the chemistry, but also showed how far he'd come from those Seventies days: "The other three guys have to be with me... they are my other powers. I couldn't be as strong without the others around... I never felt happier in my life. I wish I could have felt this way when I was younger...You think it's gonna go on forever, and then you lose it again. Nobody's gonna take it away from me now."

★ Gene, ever the conceptualist, summed up the group's overall optimism, and the reasons for returning to the face-paint: "The mood in music is down. There's a dark cloud hanging over everyone's head. There's a lot of cool stuff coming from the place where this sound originated, but there's also a lot of posing going on, people who think it's valid to live in a warm climate and dress like a lumberjack. The fakers know who they are." Simmons continued: "We're here to bring back purpose to live shows. Right now they suck a big one. We're the alternative. Good times are back."

★ However, as Kiss were trying to overturn the musical culture that had grown up since they ran the show, colleagues in waiting Bruce Kulick and Eric Singer must have been wondering what the hell fate might have in store

for them. Both on a retainer until the reunion ran its course, Bruce was kind, but realistic too about future prospects. "Well, there's six people in the band, basically," explained Kulick. "But you can't put six of us on stage, especially if they're going to perform in make-up. I always knew this was going to happen. I didn't know when exactly. But they (Gene and Paul) have decided to do it now, and they're just going to take it month by month. So, we're (he and Singer) very much a part of the band, and we've finished a record we're very proud of."

★ Ah yes, the record – *Carnival Of Souls*. Available from a good bootlegger near you. As yet, the infamous album cut by the pre-reunion line-up is still awaiting release. Obviously with the Kiss Mark One tour scheduled to proceed well into 1997 and the future beyond that as clear as fog, no-one knows quite when, or even if, we'll ever get to hear it. While Ace, Gene, Paul and Peter invade new territories daily, Bruce and Eric have had to be content to make the odd appearance at guitar exhibitions and drum clinics. They may be on a retainer wage, but their present thumb-twiddling is a criminal waste of talent and energy. They are both superb players, whose contribution to Kiss' *Revenge* was incendiary. How long will it be before they get sick of waiting and head for the hills?

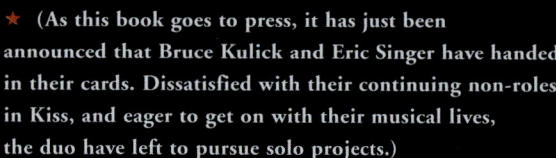

★ (As this book goes to press, it has just been announced that Bruce Kulick and Eric Singer have handed in their cards. Dissatisfied with their continuing non-roles in Kiss, and eager to get on with their musical lives, the duo have left to pursue solo projects.)

★ In Kissland, the touring proceeds apace, in America and Europe. If rumour is to be believed, it's likely the current line-up will consolidate their uncanny success with a live album and video of the current jaunt in 1997. A studio album (presumably replacing *Carnival Of Souls*) is also on the cards, but given the band's present commitments, chances are we won't hear it until 1998 at the earliest. Beyond that, we can only speculate. That Kiss have been in discussion regarding a film project is certain, and wilder talk has even linked Simmons to producing a Broadway musical based on the group's life. But that, in the main, is it. When asked about how he saw the quartet's way forward, John Stockwell, member of Kiss tribute band Destroyer, offered this prediction;

★ "They will do this for another two or three years and that'll be it. Because they will be eligible for The Rock'n'Roll Hall Of Fame in 1999. And there will be no better way than to go out on top."

★ This makes sense, as does the notion of a farewell gig on New Year's Eve, 1999. A King Hell pay-day for all concerned, it would be a fitting end to three decades on top, and ensure the legend remained indestructible for all time. But will we let them go? Arguably as important to rock culture as Elvis or The Beatles, what would a world without Kiss be like? Who would provide the circus? The drama? The sheer balls of it all? Let's face it, love them or hate them, Kiss have a purpose; They define the extremities of American rock'n'roll. In Kissland, you can voyage to the stars, play with the cat, get down with the lover or call up the devil. Pull the girl. Rock and roll all nite, and party every day. It's all yours at the drop of the needle.

★ And what of those critics who've only now seen the light? Gene Simmons provides a sneering answer: "If you're going to hate us, hate us forever."

★ The man who many see as Kiss continues: "If people look to me as a sort of leader, they're fooling themselves, 'cause I'm a complete buffoon. I enjoy being one, and nobody does it better. Paul and I feel like the two idiots in *Bill And Ted's Excellent Adventure*. Are we stupid? You bet. How about *Beavis And Butthead*? Oh, we're much much stupider than that – but we will outlast you and your kind. We are the cockroaches that will inherit the earth. Revile us – hate us – after you're long gone, we'll still be here."

★ The strangest alternative to Walt Disney you'll ever find, Kiss will prevail because they fulfil our fantasies. After all, where else are you going to find a Demon that spits blood in your face and laughs about it? An Army. A nation. We'll leave the last bit to Paul:

★ "Kiss is a life... our family is millions."

★ Revenge is sweet.

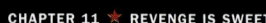

DISCOGRAPHY

SINGLES & EP'S

7" SINGLES & CASSETTE SINGLES

★ **NOTHIN' TO LOSE/**
Love Theme From Kiss
Casablanca
NEB 0004 US 1974
Casablanca
CBX503 UK 1974

★ **KISSIN' TIME/Nothin' To Lose**
Casablanca
NEB 0011 US 1974

★ **STRUTTER/100,000 Years**
Casablanca
NEB 0015 US 1974

★ **LET ME GO, ROCK'N'ROLL/**
Hotter Than Hell
Casablanca
NB 823 US 1974

★ **ROCK AND ROLL ALL NITE/**
Getaway
Casablanca
NB 829 US 1975

★ **C'MON AND LOVE ME/Getaway**
Casablanca
NB 841 US 1975

★ **ROCK AND ROLL ALL NITE (live)/**
Rock And Roll All Nite (studio)
Casablanca
NB 850 US 1975

★ **SHOUT IT OUT LOUD/Sweet Pain**
Casablanca
NB 854 US 1976

★ **FLAMING YOUTH/God Of Thunder**
Casablanca
NB 858 US 1976 (picture sleeve)

★ **DETROIT ROCK CITY/Beth**
Casablanca
NB 863 US 1976

★ **BETH/Detroit Rock City**
Casablanca
NB 863A US 1976 re-issue

★ **HARD LUCK WOMAN/Mr. Speed**
Casablanca
NB 873 US 1976
Pye CAN102 UK 1976 (picture sleeve)

★ **CALLING DR. LOVE/Take Me**
Casablanca
NB 880 US 1977

★ **THEN SHE KISSED ME/+2**
Casablanca UK 1977

★ **CHRISTINE SIXTEEN/Shock Me**
Casablanca
NB 889 US 1977
Casablanca CA 504

★ **LOVE GUN/Hooligan**
Casablanca
NB 895 US 1977

★ **SHOUT IT OUT LOUD (live)/**
Nothin' To Lose (live)
Casablanca
NB 906 US 1977

★ **ROCKET RIDE/**
Tomorrow And Tonight (live)
Casablanca
NB 915 US 1978

★ **STRUTTER '78/Shock Me**
Casablanca
NB 928 US 1978

★ **HOLD ME, TOUCH ME/Goodbye**
Casablanca
NB 940 US 1978
Casablanca
NB 940 UK 1978 (purple vinyl with picture sleeve and mask/also part of a package of 4 solo singles)

★ **NEW YORK GROOVE/Snowblind**
Casablanca
NB 941 US 1978
Casablanca
NB 941 UK 1978 (blue vinyl with picture sleeve and mask/also part of a package of 4 solo singles)

★ **RADIOACTIVE/See You In**
Your Dreams
Casablanca
NB 951 US 1978
Casablanca
NB 951 UK 1978 (red vinyl with picture sleeve and mask/also part of a package of 4 solo singles)

★ **DON'T YOU LET ME DOWN/**
Hooked On Rock And Roll
Casablanca
NB 952 US 1978
Casablanca
NB 952 UK 1978 (green vinyl with picture sleeve and mask/also part of a package of 4 solo singles)

★ **YOU MATTER TO ME/**
Hooked On Rock And Roll
Casablanca
NB 961 US 1978 (promotional)

★ **I WAS MADE FOR LOVING YOU**
(radio edit)/Hard Times (extended)
Casablanca
NB 983 US 1979
Pye CAN152 UK 1979

★ **2,000 MAN/I Was Made.../**
Sure Know Something
Casablanca
NB 1001 UK 1979 (picture sleeve)

★ **SURE KNOW SOMETHING/**
Dirty Livin'
Casablanca
NB 2205 US 1979

★ **SHANDI/She's So European**
Casablanca
2282 US 1980

★ **TOMORROW/Naked City**
Casablanca
NB 2299 US 1980

★ **A WORLD WITHOUT HEROES/**
Dark Light
Casablanca
NB 2343 US 1981

★ **A WORLD WITHOUT HEROES/**
Mr. Blackwell
Casablanca
KISS 002 UK 1981
Casablanca
KISS P002 (picture disc)

★ **I LOVE IT LOUD/Danger**
Casablanca
NB 2365 US 1982 (picture sleeve)

★ **CREATURES OF THE NIGHT/**
Rock And Roll All Nite (live)
EMI
KISS 4 811 122-7
UK 1982 (picture sleeve)

★ **LICK IT UP/**
Dance All Over Your Face
Mercury
814 671-7 US 1983

★ **LICK IT UP/**
Not For The Innocent
KISS5 UK 1983

★ **ALL HELL'S BREAKIN' LOOSE/**
Young And Wasted
Mercury
818 216-7 US 1984

★ **HEAVEN'S ON FIRE/**
Lonely Is The Hunter
Mercury
880 205-7 US 1984
VER 12 880 205-7
UK 1984 Holland (picture sleeve)

★ **THRILLS IN THE NIGHT/**
Burn Bitch, Burn
Mercury
880 535-7 US 1985 (no picture sleeve)

★ **TEARS ARE FALLING/**
Any Way You Slice It
Mercury
884 141-7 US 1985 (picture sleeve)

★ **BETH/Hard Luck Woman**
Mercury
814 303-7 US 1986
Re-issue

★ **I WAS MADE FOR LOVIN' YOU/**
R & R A N (live)
Mercury
814 304-7 US 1986
Re-issue

★ **UH! ALL NIGHT/Trial By Fire**
Mercury
884 487-7 US 1986 (picture sleeve)

★ **CRAZY, CRAZY NIGHTS/**
No, No, No
Mercury
888 796-7 US 1987 (picture sleeve)
KISS P 7 888 796-7 UK 1987
(poster bag picture sleeve)

★ **REASON TO LIVE/**
Thief In The Night
Mercury
870 022-7 US 1987 (picture sleeve)
KISS 8 870 022-7 UK 1987
(comes with patch, picture sleeve)

★ **TURN ON THE NIGHT/**
Hell Or High Water
Mercury
870 215-7 US 1988 (picture sleeve)
KISS P9 870 660-7
UK 1988 (poster bag picture sleeve)

★ **BETH/Hard Luck Woman**
Mercury
814 303-7 US 1988 (Timepieces sleeve)

★ **I WAS MADE FOR LOVIN' YOU/**
R & R A N (live)
Mercury
814 304-7 US 1988 (Timepieces sleeve)

★ **LET'S PUT THE X IN SEX/**
Calling Dr. Love
Mercury
872 246-7 US 1988 (picture sleeve)
Mercury
872 246-7 UK 1988 Holland
(different picture sleeve)
Mercury
872 246-4 US (cassette picture sleeve)

★ **HIDE YOUR HEART/Betrayed**
Mercury
876 146-7 US 1989 (no picture sleeve)
Vertigo
KISS 10 876 146-7 UK (picture sleeve also red vinyl)
Mercury 876 146-4 US (cassette picture sleeve)

★ **FOREVER (remix)/The Street**
Giveth And The Street Taketh Away
Mercury
876 716-7 US 1990 (no picture sleeve)
Mercury
876 716-4 US (cassette picture sleeve)
Vertigo
KISS 11 876 716-7 UK 1990
(picture sleeve)

★ **BETH/Hard Luck Woman**
Mercury
814 303-4 US 1990 (Timepieces cassette re-issue)

★ **RISE TO IT (full power guitar**
mix)/Silver Spoon
Mercury
875 098-7 US 1990 (no picture sleeve)
Mercury
875 098-4 US (cassette picture sleeve)

★ **GOD GAVE ROCK'N'ROLL**
TO YOU II (soundtrack edit)/
Junior's Gone Wild
East/West
A8696 UK 1991 (picture sleeve)

★ **UNHOLY/Spit**
Mercury
866 890-7 1992 (no picture sleeve)

★ **DOMINO/Carr Jam 1981**
Mercury
864 312-4 US 1992 (cassette picture sleeve)

★ **ROCK AND ROLL ALL NITE**
Mercury
1994 (7" one sided single/flipside contains the words 'It's The Music', Stupid/Very rare)

10" SINGLES

★ **HIDE YOUR HEART/Lick It Up/**
Heaven's On Fire
KISP 1010 INT 876 471-0 UK 1989
(picture disc only)

12" SINGLES

★ **THEN SHE KISSED ME/+2**
Casablanca UK 1977

★ **I WAS MADE FOR LOVIN' YOU**
(extended)
Casablanca
NB 298 US 1979 (promotional)

★ **I WAS MADE FOR LOVIN' YOU**
(extended)/Charisma
Casablanca
NBD 20169 US 1979

★ **CREATURES OF THE NIGHT/**
Rock And Roll All Nite (live)
KISS 412 UK 1982

★ **CREATURES OF THE**
NIGHT/War Machine/Rock And
Roll All Nite
Casablanca US 1982 (promotional)

★ **CREATURES OF THE NIGHT/**
Rock And Roll All Nite (live)
812 098-1 KISSD 4 UK 1982
(double grooved A-side, etched autographed B-side)

★ **KILLER/I Love It Loud/**
I Was Made For Lovin' You
Casablanca 1982

★ **LICK IT UP/Lick It Up**
PRO 229-1 US 1983 (promotional)
KPIC 5 US (promotional shaped picture disc)

★ **LICK IT UP/Not For The**
Innocent/I Still Love You
KISS 512 UK 1983

★ **ALL HELL'S BREAKIN' LOOSE/**
All Hell's Breakin' Loose
PRO 244-1 US 1984 (promotional)

★ **HEAVEN'S ON FIRE/**
Heaven's On Fire
PRO 311-1 US 1984 (promotional)

★ **HEAVEN'S ON FIRE**
Verx 12 1984 (with poster)

★ **THRILLS IN THE NIGHT/**
Thrills In The Night (radio edit)
PRO 326-1 US 1985 (promotional)

★ **TEARS ARE FALLING/**
Tears Are Falling
PRO 377-1 US 1985 (promotional)

★ **TEARS ARE FALLING/Heaven's**
On Fire (live)/Anyway You Slice It
VERTIGO
KISS 612 UK 1985

★ **UH! ALL NIGHT/Uh! All Night**
PRO 395-1 US 1986 (promotional)

★ **CRAZY, CRAZY NIGHTS/**
Crazy, Crazy Nights
PRO 531-1 US 1987 (promotional)

★ **CRAZY, CRAZY NIGHTS/**
No, No, No/-/ Lick It Up/
Uh! All Night
Vertigo
888 796-1
KISS 712 UK 1987

★ **CRAZY, CRAZY NIGHTS/**
No, No, No/Heaven's On Fire/
Tears Are Falling
Vertigo
KISS P712 UK 1987 (picture disc)

★ **REASON TO LIVE/**
Reason To Live
Mercury
PRO 559-1 US 1987 (promotional)

★ **REASON TO LIVE/Thief In**
The Night/Thrills In The Night/
Who Wants To Be Lonely
Vertigo
KISS 812 UK 1987

★ **REASON TO LIVE/Thief**
In The Night/Who Wants To Be
Lonely/Secretly Cruel
Vertigo
KISS P 812 870 058-1 UK 1987
(picture disc)

★ **TURN ON THE NIGHT/**
Turn On The Night
Mercury
PRO 572-1 US 1988 (promotional)

★ **TURN ON THE NIGHT/**
Hell Or High Water/King Of The
Mountain/Any Way You Slice It
Vertigo
KISS 912 UK 1988
Vertigo
KISS SP 912 INT 870 661-1
(picture disc)

★ **HEAVEN'S ON FIRE/**
Let's Put The X In Sex/2 others
Mercury 1988 (promotional)

★ **LET'S PUT THE X IN SEX/**
Rock And Roll All Nite/
Heaven's On Fire/Tears Are Falling
Vertigo KIZZA 1 (UK)

★ **LET'S PUT THE X IN SEX**
Mercury
US 1988 (promotional 4 versions)

★ **HIDE YOUR HEART/Betrayed/**
Boomerang
Vertigo
876 147-1
KISS X10 UK 1989

★ **FOREVER/The Street Giveth**
And The Street Taketh Away
Deuce (demo)/Strutter (demo)
Mercury
876 716-1 (US 1990)
KISXG11 (gatefold edition with discography)

★ **RISE TO IT (edit-remix)/**
Rise To It (fpgm)
Mercury 1990

★ **GOD GAVE ROCK'N'ROLL**
TO YOU II (soundtrack-edit)/
Junior's Gone Wild (King's X)/
Shout It Out (Slaughter)
UK 1991 (available as picture disc)

★ **UNHOLY/Unholy**
Mercury US 1992 (promotional)

★ **UNHOLY/Partners In Crime**
Deuce (demo)/Strutter (demo)
Mercury
KISS 1212 UK 1992 (white vinyl)

★ **UNHOLY/God Gave Rock'N'Roll**
To You II (album version)
Deuce (demo)/Strutter (demo)
Mercury 1992 (white vinyl)

VIDEOS

★ **ANIMALIZE LIVE UNCENSORED**
Detroit Rock City/Cold Gin/
Creatures Of The Night/Fits Like
A Glove/Heaven's On Fire/Thrills
In The Night/Under The Gun/
War Machine/Young And Wasted/
I Love It Loud/I Still Love You/
Love Gun/Lick It Up/Black
Diamond/Rock And Roll All Nite
Recorded live at Detroit's Cobo Hall,
8 December 1984.
RCA/Columbia Pictures Home Video
RCA 60445
Pioneer Artists (Laserdisc)
April 1985

★ **KISS MEETS THE PHANTOM
OF THE PARK**
Worldvision Home Video 9080
48CD-501 (Japan)
April 1986 (1978 made-for-TV movie)

★ **EXPOSED**
Who Wants To Be Lonely (Video '86)/
Uh! All Night (Video '86)/I Love It
Loud Live Rio de Janeiro '83/
Deuce (Live San Francisco '75)/
Strutter (Live Detroit '76)/Beth
(Live Houston '77)/Detroit Rock City
(Live Australia '80)/Tears Are Falling
(Video '85)/Lick It Up (Video '83)/
All Hell's Breakin' Loose (Video '84)/
I Love It Loud (Video '82)/
I Stole Your Love (Live Houston '77)/
Heaven's On Fire (Video '84)/Ladies'
Room (Live Houston '77)/Rock
And Roll All Nite (Live Australia '80)/
Black Diamond (Live Brazil '83)
PolyGram Video
041489/080101
May 1986

★ **CRAZY NIGHTS**
Crazy Crazy Nights (Video 1987)/
Reason To Live (Video 1987)/
Turn On The Night (Video 1988)
PolyGram Video
080301
March 1988

★ **THE INTERVIEW SESSIONS**
I.S. (no catalogue # listed) 1990
Tape of interviews with Gene Simmons
and/or Paul Stanley from 1982-87,
plus the Tomorrow Show interview from
1979, deleted and now hard to find.

★ **X-TREME CLOSE-UP**
PolyGram
KISS commercial
(1992)
Unholy
(with title credits)(video '92)
Sure Know Something
(video excerpt '79)
Watching You
(live excerpt Winterland, January '75)
**Cadillac High School
visit newsreel** *
(1976)
Black Diamond
(live excerpt Cobo Hall, January '76)
60 Minutes *
(Australia) segment (1980)
Cold Gin
(live excerpt Capital Center,
November '75)
Deuce
(live excerpt, Cobo Hall, January '76)
100,000 Years
(live excerpt, Cobo Hall, January '76)
Let Me Go Rock Rock & Roll
(live excerpt Anaheim, August '76)
Beth
(live excerpt Madison Square Garden,
February '77)
God Of Thunder
(live excerpt Budokan Hall, April '77)
Black Diamond
(live excerpt, Budokan Hall, April '77)
Love 'Em And Leave 'Em
(video '76 from Don Krishner Rock
Concert)
Hard Luck Woman
(video '76 from Don Krishner Rock
Concert)
Kiss dolls commercial *
(1978)
Kiss comics newsreel *
(1977)
I Stole Your Love
(live excerpt Magic Mtn, May '78)
Rock And Roll All Nite *
(movie opening sequence 1978)
Phantom sequence *
(1978)
I Was Made For Lovin' You
(video excerpt '79)
A World Without Heroes
(video excerpt '81)
Creatures Of The Night *
(Rockpop TV UK excerpt 1982)

Calling Dr. Love
(live excerpt, Maracana Stadium,
June '83)
War Machine
(live excerpt, Maracana Stadium
June '83)
Lick It Up
(video excerpt '83)
Let's Put The X In Sex
(video excerpt '88)
Rise To It
(video '89)
Hide Your Heart
(video '89)
Forever
(video '89)
I Just Wanna
(video excerpt '92)
God Gave Rock'N'Roll To You II * (over
closing credits)
PolyGram Video
085395
July 1992
This video has the dubious
distinction of being the most
mislabeled Kiss commercial release
ever. The above dates and concert
sites have been corrected.
Tracks marked (*) are not even listed
on the sleeve of the video!

★ **KONFIDENTIAL**
Creatures Of The Night/Deuce/
I Just Wanna/Unholy/Heaven's On
Fire/100,000 Years (Detroit '76)/
Nothin' To Lose (San Francisco '75)/
Hotter Than Hell (Detroit '76)/
Let Me Go Rock'N'Roll (Japan '77)/
Domino/Lick It Up/Forever/
Take It Off/I Love It Loud/
God Gave Rock'N'Roll To You II/
Star Spangled Banner (recorded live
in Detroit, Indianapolis & Cleveland,
27-29 November 1992)
Audio is the same as on *Alive III*.
PolyGram Video
400876033
Released 20 July 1993

★ **KISS MY A***
Parasite
(live Winterland, January '75)
Do You Love Me?
(live Madison Square Garden,
February '77)
Radioactive
(live Capital Center, July '79)
Move On
(live Capital Center, July '79)
Kiss dolls commercial *
1978
America's Top-10 interview *
1981
Love Gun
(live The Palace of Auburn Hills,
November '92)
New York Groove
(live Capital Center, July '79)
Kiss radio commercial *
(1977)
SNL sketch *
(1977)
Kiss Your Face commercial *
(1978)
She
(by Anthrax 1994)
Dick Clark's Golden Greats segment *
(1986)
Makin' Love
(live Madison Square Garden,
February '77)
Christine Sixteen
(by Gin Blossoms 1994)
Rock And Roll Over commercial *
(version 2, 1976)
Double Platinum commercial outtake *
(1978)
Channel 6 TV (France) segment *
(1989)
I Love It Loud
(Italian TV, November '82)
Alive II commercial *
(version 1, 1977)
C'mon And Love Me
(live Cobo Hall, January '76)
Late Night with Conan O'Brien *
segment (1993)
Dynasty album
(tour commercial excerpt 1979)
Hooligan
(live The Summit, September '77)
Shock Me
(live The Summit, September '77)
I
(Studio 54, December 1981)
Take Me Rehearsal
(November '76)
Hotter Than Hell commercial *
(1974)
WOR-TV news segment *
(1993)
Solo albums commercial *
(1978)
She
(live Cobo Hall, January '76)
Black Diamond
(live Cobo Hall, January '76)
PolyGram Video
800632349
Released August 1994
Video edited by Jerry Behrens and
Kiss. Entries with a (*) are not listed
on the sleeve for the video.

★ **INSIDE THE CASBAH:
A HISTORY OF CASABLANCA
RECORD AND FILMWORKS**
C'mon And Love Me
(video 1975)
Rock and Roll Over
(commercial, version 1, 1976)
Love Gun
(commercial 1977)
Alive II
(promo with excerpts from
Detroit Rock City/Rockin' In The
U.S.A./Love Gun/Beth/Rocket Ride/
Shout It Out Loud/Alive II
(commercial, version 1, 1977)
Alive II
(commercial, version 2, 1977)
Double Platinum
(commercial 1978)
Solo Albums
(commercial 1978)
Dynasty
(commercial, version 1, 1979)
Dynasty
(commercial, version 2, 1979)
Dynasty
(tour promo with excerpts from
Sure Know Something and I Was
Made For Lovin' You
Sure Know Something
(video 1979)
Casablanca Newsreel
(on solo albums release 1979)
Rock Steady Productions
516-588-6600
April 1995
About half of the tape's 50 minutes
are dedicated to Kiss. All clips
are in perfect condition, as opposed
to the Kiss My Ass ones.
Other performers include Donna
Summer, Parliament and Village
People. Dedicated to Joyce Bogart.

KISS ALBUMS

Albums marked † are not part of the 'official' KISS discography, as they are either promos or non-US releases

★ **WICKED LESTER**
Sweet Ophelia/Keep Me Waiting/
Love Her All I Can/Simple Type/She/
Too Many Mondays/In The Darkness/
When The Bell Rings/Molly
Epic/CBS (catalogue # n/a)
Unreleased 1972

★ **UNTITLED**
Deuce/Cold Gin/Strutter/
Watching You/Black Diamond
Kiss' first demo (no record label)
Unreleased 1973

★ **KISS**
Strutter/Nothin' To Lose/
Firehouse/Cold Gin/Let Me
Know/Deuce/Love Theme From Kiss/
100,000 Years/Black Diamond
Casablanca/Warner
NBLP 9001 (US)
Released February 1974

★ **KISS**
Strutter/Nothin' To Lose/Firehouse/
Cold Gin/Let Me Know/Kissin' Time/
Deuce/Love Theme From Kiss/
100,000 Years/Black Diamond
Casablanca/Warner
NBLP 7001 (US)
Casablanca/Phonogram
6399-057 (Europe)
VIP 6326, P33C-20003, 22S-1 (Japan)
Casablanca/PolyGram
824-146-1/7
July 1974
Re-issue July 1985
CD re-issue July 1987

★ **HOTTER THAN HELL**
Got To Choose/Parasite/
Goin' Blind/Hotter Than Hell/
Let Me Go/Rock'N'Roll All The Way/
Watchin' You/Mainline/
Comin' Home/Strange Ways
Casablanca/Warner
NBLP 7006 (US)
Casablanca/Phonogram
6399-058 (Europe)
VIP 6340, P33C-20004, 22S-2 (Japan)
Casablanca/PolyGram
824-147-1/4
Casablanca/PolyGram
824-147
October 1974
Re-issue July 1985
CD re-issue July 1987

★ **DRESSED TO KILL**
Room Service/Two Timer/
Ladies In Waiting/Getaway/Rock
Bottom/C'mon And Love Me/
Anything For My Baby/She/Love Her
All I Can/Rock And Roll All Nite
Casablanca/Warner
NBLP 7016 (US)
Casablanca/Phonogram
6399-059 (Europe)
VIP 6396, P33C-20005, 22S-3 (Japan)
Casablanca/PolyGram
824-148-1/4
March 1975
Re-issue July 1985
CD re-issue July 1987

★ **ALIVE!**
Deuce/Strutter/Got To Choose/
Hotter Than Hell/Firehouse/
Nothin' To Lose/C'mon And Love Me/
Parasite/She/Watchin' You/
100,000 Years/Black Diamond/
Rock Bottom/Cold Gin/Rock And
Roll All Nite/Let Me Go/Rock'N'Roll
Casablanca/Warner
NBLP 7020 (US)
Casablanca/Phonogram
6640 026 (Europe)
VIP 9515/16 (Japan)
Casablanca/PolyGram
822-780-1/4
September 1975
Re-issue July 1985
CD re-issue July 1987

★ **DESTROYER**
Detroit Rock City/King Of The
Night Time World/God Of Thunder/
Great Expectations/Flaming Youth/
Sweet Pain/Shout It Out Loud/Beth/
Do You Love Me (Untitled Track)
Casablanca/Warner
NBLP 7025 (US)
Casablanca/Phonogram
6399-064 (Europe)
VIP 6435 & SWX 6268, P33C-20006,
22S-4 (Japan)
Casablanca/PolyGram
824-149-1/4
Casablanca/PolyGram
824-149-2
March 1976
Re-issue July 1985
CD re-issue July 1987

★ **SPECIAL KISS TOUR ALBUM †**
Beth/Do You Love Me/
Flaming Youth/Detroit Rock City
Casablanca/Warner
Kiss '76 (US)
June 1976

★ **THE ORIGINALS †**
Kiss' first three albums
in one package:
KISS
HOTTER THAN HELL
DRESSED TO KILL
Casablanca/Warner
NBLP 7032
July 1976
Issued in Japan VIP 5504-5
January 1978

★ **ROCK AND ROLL OVER**
I Want You/Take Me/Calling
Dr. Love/Ladies Room/Baby Driver/
Love 'Em And Leave 'Em/Mr. Speed/
See You In Your Dreams/
Hard Luck Woman/Makin' Love
Casablanca
NBLP 7037 (US)
Casablanca/Phonogram
6399-060 (Europe)
VIP 6376, P33C-20007, 22S-5 (Japan)
Casablanca/PolyGram
824-150-1/4
Casablanca/PolyGram
824-150-2
November 1976
Re-issue July 1985
CD re-issue July 1987

★ **ROCK AND ROLL OVER –
SPECIAL EDITION †**
I Want You/Hard Luck Woman/
Take Me/Baby Driver/Love 'Em
And Leave 'Em
Casablanca
NBLP 7037 DJ (US)
November 1976

★ **LOVE GUN**
I Stole Your Love/Christine
Sixteen/Got Love For Sale/
Shock Me/Tomorrow And Tonight/
Love Gun/Hooligan/Almost Human/
Plaster Caster/Then She Kissed Me
Casablanca
NBLP 7057 (US)
Casablanca/Phonogram
6399-063 (Europe)
VIP 6435, P33C-20008, 22S-6 (Japan)
Casablanca/PolyGram
824-151-1/4
June 1977
Re-issue July 1985
CD re-issue July 1987

★ **KISS ALIVE II**
Detroit Rock City/King Of The
Night Time World/Ladies Room/
Makin' Love/Love Gun/Calling Dr.
Love/Christine Sixteen/Shock Me/
Hard Luck Woman/Tomorrow And
Tonight/I Stole Your Love/Beth/
God Of Thunder/I Want You/Shout
It Out Loud/All American Man/
Rockin' In The USA/Larger Than Life/
Rocket Ride/Any Way You Want It
Casablanca
NBLP 7076 (US)
Casablanca/Phonogram
6685-043 (Europe)
VIP 9529/30 (Japan)
Casablanca/PolyGram
822-781-1/4
Casablanca/PolyGram
822-781-2
October 1977
Re-issue July 1985
CD re-issue July 1987

★ **DOUBLE PLATINUM**
Strutter '78/Do You Love Me/
Hard Luck Woman/Calling Dr. Love/
Let Me Go/Rock'N'Roll/Love Gun/
God Of Thunder/Firehouse/
Hotter Than Hell/I Want You Deuce/
100,000 Years/Detroit Rock City/
Rock Bottom (Intro)/She/
Rock And Roll All Nite/Beth/
Makin' Love/C'mon And Love
Me/Cold Gin/Black Diamond
Casablanca
NBLP 7100 (US)
Casablanca/Phonogram
6641-907 (Europe)
VIP 9549 (Japan)
Casablanca/PolyGram
824-155-1/4
Casablanca/PolyGram
824-155-2
April 1978
Re-issue July 1985
CD re-issue July 1987

★ **A TASTE OF PLATINUM †**
Strutter '78/Do You Love Me/
Love Gun/Firehouse
Casablanca
NB 20128 (US)
March 1978

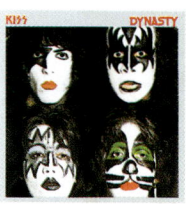

★ **DYNASTY**
I Was Made For Lovin' You/
2,000 Man/Sure Know Something/
Dirty Livin'/Charisma/Magic Touch/
Hard Times/X-Ray Eyes/
Save Your Love
Casablanca
NBLP 7152 (US)
Casablanca/Phonogram
9128-024 (Europe)
P33C-20009, 22S-11 (Japan)
Casablanca/PolyGram
812-770-1/4
Casablanca/PolyGram
812-770-2
May 1979
Re-issue July 1985
CD re-issue July 1987

★ **UNMASKED**
Is That You?/Shandi/Talk To Me/
Naked City/What Makes The World
Go 'Round Tomorrow/Two Sides
Of The Coin/She's So European/
Easy As It Seems/Torpedo Girl/
You're All That I Want
Casablanca
NBLP 7225 (US)
Casablanca/Phonogram
6302-032 (Europe)
VIP 25S-3, P33C-20010, 25S-3 (Japan)
Casablanca/PolyGram
800-041-1/4
Casablanca/PolyGram
800-041-2
May 1980
Re-issue July 1985
CD re-issue July 1987

★ **(MUSIC FROM) THE ELDER**
The Oath/Fanfare/Just A Boy/
Dark Light/Only You/Under The Rose/
A World Without Heroes/
Mr. Blackwell/Escape From The
Island/Odyssey/I
Casablanca
NBLP 7261 (US)
Casablanca/Phonogram
6302-163 (Europe)
Casablanca/PolyGram
6480-071 (US export)
November 1981
CD re-issue May 1989

★ **(MUSIC FROM) THE ELDER**
Fanfare/Just A Boy/Odyssey/
Only You/Under The Rose/Dark Light/
A World Without Heroes/The Oath/
Mr. Blackwell/I
(Japan only)
Polystar 28S-23
Casablanca P33C-20011
November 1981
CD re-issue 1988

★ **KISS KILLERS**
I'm A Legend Tonight/Down On
Your Knees/Cold Gin/Love Gun/
Shout It Out Loud (remix)/Sure
Know Something/Nowhere To Run/
Partners In Crime/Detroit Rock
City/God Of Thunder/I Was Made
For Lovin' You/Rock And Roll All
Nite (live)
Released everywhere except US
and Canada.
Casablanca/Phonogram
6302-193
Polydor
812 771-1/2/4
May 1982
Re-issue 1989

★ **CREATURES OF THE NIGHT**
Creatures Of The Night/Saint And
Sinner/Keep Me Comin'/Rock And
Roll Hell/Danger/I Love It Loud/
I Still Love You/Killer/War Machine
Casablanca
NBLP 7270 (US)
Casablanca/Phonogram
6302-219 (Europe)
P33C-20013, 28S-138 (Japan)
Mercury/PolyGram 824-154-1/4
Mercury/PolyGram 824-154-2
October 1982
Re-released October 1995
CD re-issue July 1987

★ **HOTTER THAN METAL†**
Deuce/Strutter/Got To Choose/
Hotter Than Hell/Firehouse/Nothin'
To Lose/C'mon And Love Me/
Parasite/She
(Holland only)
Phonogram (catalogue # n/a)
1982

★ **SUPER STAR†**
Deuce/Strutter/Got To Choose/
Hotter Than Hell/Firehouse/Nothin'
To Lose/C'mon And Love Me/
Parasite/She
(Italy only)
Polygram
Released 1982

★ **LICK IT UP**
Exciter/Not For The Innocent/
Lick It Up/Young And Wasted/
Gimme More/All Hell's Breakin'
Loose/A Million To One/Fits Like
A Glove/Dance All Over Your Face/
And On The 8th Day
Mercury/PolyGram
814-297-1/2/4
Casablanca/Polystar
28S-181 (Japan with makeup cover)
P33C-20014 (Japan CD)
September 1983

★ **ANIMALIZE**
I've Had Enough (Into The Fire)/
Heaven's On Fire/Burn Bitch Burn/
Get All You Can Take/Lonely Is
The Hunter/Under The Gun/
Thrills In The Night/While The City
Sleeps/Murder In High Heels
Mercury/PolyGram
822-495-1/2/4, P33C-20015,
28SA-250 (Japan)
September 1984

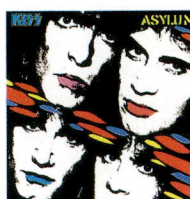

★ **ASYLUM**
King Of The Mountain/Any Way
You Slice It/Who Wants To Be Lonely/
Trial By Fire/I'm Alive/Love's A
Deadly Weapon/Tears Are Falling/
Secretly Cruel/Radar For Love/
Uh! All Night
Mercury/PolyGram
826-099-1/2/4
September 1985

★ **CRAZY NIGHTS**
Crazy Crazy Nights/I'll Fight
Hell To Hold You/Bang Bang You/
No, No, No/Hell Or High Water/
My Way/When Your Walls Come
Down/Reason To Live/Good Girl
Gone Bad/Turn On The Night/
Thief In The Night
Mercury/PolyGram
832-626-1/2/4
Mercury/PolyGram
832-903-1 (German picture disc)
September 1987

★ **CHIKARA†**
Japanese only compilation with
three new remixes 'Creatures Of The
Night'/'I Love It Loud/War Machine'
and the 12" single version of 'I
Was Made For Lovin' You'.
(Japan only)
Polystar
P30R-20008
May 1988

★ **SMASHES, THRASHES & HITS**
Let's Put The X In Sex/
(You Make Me) Rock Hard/
Love Gun (remix)/Detroit Rock City
(remix)/I Love It Loud (remix)/
Deuce (remix)/Lick It Up/
Heaven's On Fire/Calling Dr. Love
(remix)/Strutter (remix)/Beth/
Tears Are Falling/I Was Made For
Lovin' You/Rock And Roll All Nite
(remix)/Shout It Out Loud (remix)
Mercury/PolyGram
836-427-1/2/4 (US)
Pye 2006 (UK red vinyl LP)
November 1988

★ **SMASHES, THRASHES & HITS**
(Europe only)
Different versions of this album
were released. Only the CD contains
'Calling Dr. Love' (marked as a
bonus track), and it is not the same
remixed version that appeared on the
US album.
Vertigo/Phonogram
836-759-1/2/4
November 1988

★ **SMASHES, THRASHES & HITS:
15 YEARS OF KISSTORY†**
Same as above but this album
came in a gatefold sleeve and
included a bio-essay by John David
Kalodner, discography, videography,
8 photos and a two-sided picture
disc (with the album cover on one side
and a 1976 shot of the band on
the other).
Mercury/PolyGram
836-887-1 (picture Disc) (US)
January 1989

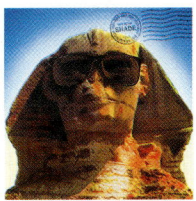

★ **HOT IN THE SHADE**
Rise To It/Betrayed/Hide Your
Heart/Prisoner Of Love/Read My
Body/Love's A Slap In The Face/
Forever/Silver Spoon/Cadillac
Dreams/King Of Hearts/The Street
Giveth And The Street Taketh Away/
You Love Me To Hate You/
Somewhere Between Heaven And
Hell/Little Caesar/Boomerang
Mercury/PolyGram
838-913-1/2/4
October 1989

★ **FIRST KISS LAST LICKS†**
Love's A Slap In The Face/
Betrayed/Prisoner Of Love/
The Street Giveth And The Street
Taketh Away/Nowhere To Run
(1989 remix)/Partners In Crime
(1989 remix)/Deuce (demo)/
Strutter (demo)
Mercury/PolyGram
PRO 792-1
February 1990

★ **FIRST KISS†**
The first four Kiss albums
packaged together.
Mercury
846-766-2
October 1990

★ **REVENGE**
Unholy/Take It Off/Tough Love/
Spit/God Gave Rock'N'Roll To
You II/Domino/Heart Of Chrome/
Thou Shalt Not/Every Time I Look
At You/Paralyzed/I Just Wanna/
Carr Jam 1981
Mercury/PolyGram
848-037-2/4/5 (5 stands for DCC)
Mercury/Nippon-Phonogram
PHCR 36 (Japan, special edition)
Mercury/Nippon-Phonogram
PHCR-1169 (Japan)
May 1992

★ **ALIVE III**
Creatures Of The Night/Deuce/
I Just Wanna/Unholy/Heaven's On
Fire/Watchin' You/Domino/
I Was Made For Lovin' You/I Still
Love You/Rock And Roll All Nite/
Lick It Up/Forever/I Love It Loud/
Detroit Rock City/God Gave
Rock'N'Roll To You II/Star Spangled
Banner
(North America only)
Mercury/PolyGram
514-777-2/4/5
May 1993

★ **ALIVE III**
Includes 'Take It Off' not available
on North American CD pressings.
Mercury/Phonogram
514-827-2/4
Mercury/PolyGram
514-827-1 (US coloured vinyl)
May 1993
Vinyl Released May 1994

★ **ALIVE THE TRILOGY†**
Limited edition boxed set containing
all the live albums.
Mercury 5CD Boxed Set
September 1993

★ **MTV UNPLUGGED**
Comin' Home/Plaster Caster/
Goin' Blind/Do You Love Me/Domino/
Sure Know Something/A World
Without Heroes/Rock Bottom/
See You Tonight/I Still Love You/
Every Time I Look At You/2,000 Man/
Beth/Nothin' To Lose/Rock And
Roll All Nite
Mercury/Polygram
528-950-1/4/2
March 1996

★ **YOU WANTED THE BEST,
YOU GOT THE BEST !!**
Room Service*/Two Timer*/
Let Me Know*/Rock Bottom/
Parasite/Firehouse/I Stole Your Love/
Callin' Dr. Love/Take Me*/Shout It
Out Loud/Beth/Rock And Roll All
Nite/Bonus track: Kiss Tells All -
An interview with Jay Leno
(*live version previously unreleased)
Mercury/Polygram
532 741-2
June 1996

SOLO ALBUMS

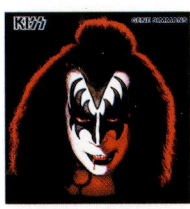

★ **GENE SIMMONS**
Radioactive/Burning Up With Fever/
See You Tonite/Tunnel Of Love/
True Confessions/Living In Sin/
Always Near You/Nowhere To Hide/
Man Of 1,000 Faces/Mr. Make
Believe/See You In Your Dreams/
When You Wish Upon A Star
Casablanca
NBLP 7120 (US)
Casablanca NBPIX 7120 (picture disc)
VIP 6578 (Japan)
Casablanca/PolyGram
826-239-1/2/4
September 1978
Re-issue April 1988

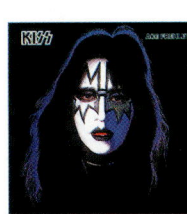

★ **ACE FREHLEY**
Rip It Out/Speedin' Back To
My Baby/Snow Blind/Ozone/
What's On Your Mind?/New York
Groove/I'm In Need Of Love/
Wiped-Out/Fractured Mirror
Casablanca NBLP 7121 (US)
Casablanca NBPIX 7121 (picture disc)
VIP 6579 (Japan)
Casablanca/PolyGram
826-916-1/2/4
September 1978
Re-issue April 1988

★ **PETER CRISS**
I'm Gonna Love You/You Matter
To Me/Tossin' And Turnin'/
Don't You Let Me Down/That's The
Kind Of Sugar Papa Likes/Easy
Thing/Rock Me/Baby/Kiss The Girl
Goodbye/Hooked On Rock And Roll/
I Can't Stop The Rain
Casablanca
NBLP 7122 (US)
Casablanca
NBPIX 7122 (picture disc)
VIP 6580 (Japan)
Casablanca/PolyGram
826-917-1/24
September 1978
Re-issue April 1988

★ **PAUL STANLEY**
Tonight You Belong To Me/
Move On/Ain't Quite Right/
Wouldn't You Like To Know Me/
Take Me Away (Together As One)/
It's Alright, Hold Me/Touch Me/
(Think Of Me When We're Apart)/
Love In Chains/Goodbye
Casablanca
NBLP 7123 (US)
Casablanca
NBPIX 7123 (picture disc)
VIP 6577 (Japan)
Casablanca/PolyGram
826-915-1/2/4
September 1978
Re-issue April 1988

★ **SOLO ALBUM SAMPLER†**
Don't You Let Me Down/
You Matter To Me/New York Groove/
Fractured Mirror/See You Tonite/
Radioactive/Hold Me/Touch Me/
Take Me Away (Together As One)
Casablanca
NB 20137 DJ (US)
September 1978

★ **BEST OF SOLO ALBUMS†**
New York Groove/Rip It Out/
Speedin' Back To My Baby/
You Matter To Me, Tossin'
And Turnin'/Hooked On Rock And
Roll/Radioactive/Mr. Make
Believe/See You In Your Dreams/
Tonight You Belong To Me/
Move On/Hold Me, Touch Me
(Europe only)
Casablanca/Phonogram
6302-060
January 1981

★ HARD TO BELIEVE:
A KISS COVERS ALBUM
Detroit Rock City/Bullet Lavolta/
Parasite/Smelly Tounges/Snowblind/
Skin Yard/Deuce/Hellmen/Christine
Sixteen/Ali, Calling Dr. Love/
Hullabaloo/God Of Thunder (+)/
The Melvins/Beth/Coffin Break/Rip
It Out/Chemical People/I Want You/
King Snake Roost/Do You Love Me?/
Nirvana/Lick It Up/The Hard Ons,
Is That You? (+)/Girl Monstar/Sure
Know Something (+)/Whipper
(Featuring Rock Hard)/Love Gun (+)/
Surfin' Caesars/War Machine (+)/
The Instigators/Deuce (+)/
Treepeople/Makin' Love (+)/Thrust/
Charisma (+)/Plunderers/Beth/
The Hard Ons
C/Z CZ024
June 1990

★ FLAMING YOUTH:
A NORWEGIAN TRIBUTE TO KISS
Deuce – Graceland
Strutter – Grunt People
w/Linda Johansen
Love Gun – Ramjam
Mainline – Mother's Love
Parasite – Hedge Hog
Tomorrow – The Stuck
Calling Dr. Love – Blant De Primitive
Shock Me – Motorpsycho w/Dag
Ingebrigtsen
Beth – Gartnerlosjen
She – Paraplegic
Strange Ways – Spacemen Stiff
Watchin' You – Lost At Last
Shout It Out Loud – Dumdum Boys
Cold Gin – Muck
I Was Made For Lovin' You –
The Jungle Medics
Rock And Roll All Nite –
Cosmic Dropouts
Greetings To Paul (+) – Bare Egil Band
REC 90/Groovy MNM/
Voices of Wonder RID-011 (Norway)
May 1994

★ KISS MY ASS:
CLASSIC KISS REGROOVED
Deuce –
Lenny Kravitz w/Stevie Wonder
Hard Luck Woman –
Garth Brooks w/Kiss
She – Anthrax
Christine Sixteen – Gin Blossoms
Rock And Roll All Nite – Toad The Wet
Sprocket
Calling Dr. Love – Shandi's
Addiction/Going Blind – Dinosaur Jr.
Strutter – Extreme
Plaster Caster – The Lemonheads
Detroit Rock City –
Mighty Mighty Bosstones
Black Diamond – Yoshiki
Unholy (+) – Die Artze
Mercury/PolyGram
314-522-123-1 (red vinyl)
Mercury/PolyGram
314-522-393-2/4 (censored)
Mercury/PolyGram
314-522-123-2/4 (uncensored)
Mercury/PolyGram
314-522-476-2/4 (outside US)
June 1994 (track 12 only available
on US vinyl and non-US CDs)

★ SPACEWALK –
A TRIBUTE TO ACE FREHLEY
Deuce - Marty Freidman
Shock Me - Gilby Clarke
Rip It Out - Scott Ian
Hard Luck Woman - Ron Young &
Jeff Watson
Snowblind - Snake Sabo
Rock Bottom - Sebastian Bach
Parasite - Tracii Guns
Cold Gin - John Norum
New York Groove - Bruce Bouillet
Fractured Mirror - Dimebag Darrell
Take Me To The City - Ace Frehley
Rock/Triage Records
Derc - 076e 1996

★ ROCK AND ROLL AIN'T OVER –
A TRIBUTE TO KISS
A European homage to Kiss just
out as this book went to press.
Featuring mainly Swedish and
Norweigan acts such as Transport
League and Breakfast Conspiracy
covering tunes as diverse as
'I Stole Your Love' and 'War Machine'.
British Kiss tribute band Dressed
To Kill cover 'C'mon And Love Me'.
Tribute Troo6 1996

TRIBUTE ALBUMS

OTHER KISS-RELATED RECORDS

PETER CRISS

ALBUMS

★ CHELSEA: 'CHELSEA'
Rollin' Along/Let's Call It A Day/
Silver Lining/All American Boy/Hard
Rock Music/Ophelia, Long River/
Grace/Polly You/Good Company
Decca
DI 75262
Released 1971

★ OUT OF CONTROL
By Myself/In Trouble Again/
Where Will They Run/I Found Love/
There's Nothing Better/Out Of
Control/Words/You Better Run/
My Life/Feel Like Letting Go
Casablanca
NBLP 7240
Mercury/Phonogram
6302-065 (Europe)
VIP 22S-14 (Japan)
June 1980

★ LET ME ROCK YOU
Let It Go/Tears/Move On Over/
Jealous Guy/Destiny/Some Kinda'
Hurricane/Let Me Rock You/
First Day In The Rain/Feel Like
Heaven/Bad Boys
Casablanca
6302-194 1982

★ CRISS: 'CRISS'
The Cat/Show Me/Good Times/
What You're Doin'/Beth
Tony Nicole
0004-25E
December 1993

★ CRISS: CAT # 1
Bad Attitude/Walk The Line/
The Truth/Bad People Burn In Hell/
Show Me/Good Times/Strike/
Blue Moon Over Brooklyn/Down With
The Sun/We Want You/Beth
Tony Nicole
Tony Records
0004-2 1994
Ace Frehley appears on tracks on
1, 2 & 8.

SINGLES

★ Tears/Jealous Guy
Casablanca 1982

★ Bad Attitude
Tony Nicole 0004-2A 1994

ACE FREHLEY

ALBUMS

★ MOLIMO
RCA
(no catalogue # available)
Unreleased 1972
First Ace Frehley on vinyl.
Album is extremely rare.

★ CRAZY JOE AND
THE VARIABLE SPEED BAND:
'CRAZY JOE AND THE VARIABLE...'
Casablanca
NBLP/5 7254 1981
Eugene – track co-written and
co-produced by Ace Frehley.
He also plays synth drums on it,
as well as another track The Gay
Ranchero.

★ DEMO
Audio/Video/The Hurt Is On/
I Got The Touch/Rock or Be Rocked/
Remember Me/Baby It's You/
Gotta Find A Party/The Girl Can't
Dance
(no record label)
Unreleased 1984

★ WE GOT YOUR ROCK
Dancing With Danger/Into The
Night/Angel/Back On The Streets/
Rock Or Be Rocked/Give It To Me
Anyway/Stranger In A Strange Land/
Dolls/Animal/Ecstacy We Got
Your Rock
(no record label)
Unreleased 1985

★ FREHLEY'S COMET
Rock Soldiers/Breakout/Into The
Night/Something Moved/We Got Your
Rock/Love Me Right/Calling To You/
Dolls/Stranger In A Strange Land/
Fractured Too (Instrumental)
Megaforce Worldwide
81749-1/2/4 1987

★ FREHLEY'S COMET:
'LIVE +1'
Rip It Out/Breakout/Something
Moved/Rocket Ride/Words Are Not
Enough (studio)
Megaforce Worldwide
81826-1/2/4 1988

★ FREHLEY'S COMET:
'SECOND SIGHTING'
Insane/Time Ain't Runnin' Out/
Dancin' With Danger/It's Over Now/
Loser In A Fight/Juvenile Delinquent/
Fallen Angel/Separate/New Kind
Of Lover/The Acorn Is Spinning
Megaforce Worldwide
81862-1/2/4 1988

★ TROUBLE WALKIN'
Shot Full Of Rock/Do Ya/Five Card
Stud/Hide Your Heart/Lost In Limbo/
Trouble Walkin'/2 Young 2 Die/
Back To School/Remember Me/
Fractured III
Megaforce Worldwide
82042-1/2/4 1989
Both Sebastian Bach and Rachel Bolan
from Skid Row appear on this release.

★ FREHLEY'S COMET: LIVE +4
Rip It Out/Something Moved/
Cold Gin/Shock Me/Breakout/
Rocket Ride/Into The Night/
Rock Soldiers/Insane/It's Over Now
Atlantic Video 50131-3 1988.
Filmed live at the Hammersmith
Odeon, London 19 March 1988.

★ ACE FREHLEY:
ACEVISION VOLUME 1
Shock Me/Rip It Out/Rocket Ride/
Breakout/Cold Gin/New York Groove/
Parasite/Shot Full of Rock/
Rock Soldiers
(no catalogue #) 1994
Filmed during Ace's Just 4 Fun tour,
Spring 1993.
Available only at live shows and
through his fan club Rock Soldiers.

SINGLES

★ Rock Soldiers
Megaforce Worldwide 1987

★ Calling To You
Megaforce Worldwide 1987

★ Into The Night
Megaforce Worldwide 1987

★ Insane
Megaforce Worldwide 1988

★ Separate
Megaforce Worldwide 1988

★ Do Ya
Megaforce Worldwide 1989

★ Do Ya
Megaforce Worldwide
PR 3010-2 CD-promo 1989